THE DOWNFALL OF MANIFESTO THE GREAT

A Sci-Fi Comedy Where Women Revolt

KERRIE NOOR

CONTENTS

Glossary   vii
Meet The Gang   ix
The Downfall of Manifesto the Great   xi

Part One   1

1. The Orphan   2
   "In the beginning, there was Beryl."—Verruca

2. The Library   6
   *"Spying is not an easy thing to do in a wheelchair, no matter how
   motorized."—The chairman*

3. Jack and John   10
   *"It is no-nonsense bossing that is the making of a ruler."—Scribed at the feet
   of a headless statue*

4. Aggie   13
   "The handing over of things has nothing to do with hands."—Aggie

5. The Speech   19
   "Spying is easy in a wheelchair; no one sees you."—The Librarian

6. Gristle   26
   "Never judge a sandwich by its crust."—Jack

7. The Turtle   30
   "Never judge a rope by its length."—The unknown cleaner

8. Ashes to Ashes   35
   "Talking with eyes is the beginning of love."—Tork

9. The Shed   40
   "The scent of the past jump-starts a memory better than any photo."—Jack

10. The Oaf of a Footman   43
    *"A woman with time on her hands is a revolution waiting to happen."—
    The Librarian*

11. Cocktails   49
    *"The memory of a computer is useless without the password."—The Mae
    West robot*

12. Oranges and Socks   53
    *"The tossing of a wig is on par with the tossing of a bra."—The Mae West
    robot*

13. The Lowering of the Flag   58
    *"Playing requires imagination; imagination while obeying is optional."—
    The unknown cleaner*

14. Another Shed   63
    *"A robot that knows the ropes is likely to be a Mae West prototype."—The
    Mae West robot*

15. The Canteen 69
"The best way to hold a robot is with lubrication."—The Mae West robot

16. Caught 74
"Never judge a robot by its quotes."—The Mae West robot

17. The Chairman 78
"From an early age, Manifesto the Great loved to write things, and, despite technology, did it with a quill. The feather tip made him happy; others said it made him look mad."—Aggie's Greenhouse Guide

18. Diversions 82
"An uprising by any other name still requires paperwork."—Fanny

19. Sneaking Around 87
"A memo by any name still requires that sticky bit."—Beryl

20. The Marketplace 91
"They didn't bank on the Mae West robot. No one did."—Footman unknown

21. The Smoking Jacket 96
"Manifesto the Great was a short and speedy man; foolish dreams ran from him quicker than a running tap."—The footman in tight trousers

22. Graffiti 101
"I only have yes-men around me who needs no men."—The chairman, stealing from the real Mae West

23. Tunnels and Petticoats 106
"Soon, bed-diving, like fishing, barbecuing, and a good old-fashioned chase-the-chicken-around-the-field, was off the table."—Manifesto the Great

24. Wielding and Mops 111
"An obelisk does not live up to its complicated spelling."—Fanny

25. Statues and Thighs 116
"They can lead us to the kitchen, but they'll never make us swallow."—Fanny

26. The Courtyard of Greatness 122
"Some would say foreplay has little to do with play; others would disagree."—Reader

Part Two 128
Ten years later

27. Lipsticks and Wigs 129
"At the end, there was Beryl."—Verruca

28. Whiteboard 133
"Sperm gave men the ability to lift, yell, and make things rise, while ovaries made women cry at the oddest of things and burn toast."—The Librarian

29. Memories 138
"The Petri was the great hope of many men whose women seemed to always have a headache."—Manifesto the Great

30. Verruca 143
"Looking the part is not the same as being the part."—Manifesto the Great's footman

31. Starfish 147
"A little incognito never harmed anyone."—Fanny

32. Meditations and Bunions   151
"Sometimes a ruler needs a gentle push of his perch."—LM-2

33. TNT   154
"Her mother was a servicer, which Beryl happily said until she realized what it meant."—The Librarian

The Beginning of the End   159

The Legacy Of Manifesto The Great   161

A Note From The Author   167

Other Books by Kerrie Noor   169

GLOSSARY

Four Legged-Creatures :- a much talked about myth until the spaceship landed, the idea of a creature with four legs was as plausible as a woman ruling the planet.

Sex For Procreation Treaty:- unlike the quickly put together treatise of "your uterus - our survival" and "one shag one night," the sex for procreation treaty was an idea bandied about the spaceship by Wife-ie to give hope; no one thought that once landed it would come into force.

Sphere Of Energy : - a closely guarded secret handed down from Hubbie to his son. Instructions on how to light a fire without matches folded up in an empty match box; along with a few other handy formulas.

Wife-ie's Stretch and Breathe Pose: - considered by many to be the beginnings of robotic yoga, not to mention the much-whispered tantric seduction Aggie was famed for.

Bed-diving : - an act that requires neither beds nor the art of diving.

Nurturing Shed : - the tools of a nurturing shed are kept hidden from all until needed—once seen, a woman rarely opens her legs again.

The Ownership Act : - the sort of marriage most civilisations were built on.

Reflectors: - early mirrors which men blamed for the dissatisfaction of their women.

The Outlands: - a bit like the Australian outback, but with out kangaroos.

Talking Stick: - passed around like a good old fashion fag. The holding of the stick meant you had the floor and could "talk the hind leg of a four legged-creature—ad infinitum," except some took the "ad infinitum" literally, leading to the tossing of said "talking stick.".

In the end, the talking stick became as obsolete as arm wrestling, finding a home in the museum of field workers, a museum with no entrance fee as there is bugger all to see.

Turtles: - the great innovation of those in the art centre, where they grew tired of transporting things, little did they know where it would led.

MEET THE GANG

Beryl : - a woman from nowhere who finally makes it almost to the top.

The Readers: - readers under the chairman's rule, rather than that of Manifesto the Great, the leader.

Jack and John : -forgotten scientist of the Institute who can't help themselves when it comes to fertilisation, of the Petri dish kind.

Mae West robots: - famed for their massages, which, like marmite are either loved or loathed.

Turtle robots :- designed to carry and transport, earning the designer a statue in the courtyard of greatness. His statue was soon defaced once the design fault of roaring and stomping was discovered.

Bette: - a cleaner with high ambitions and a glare to back it up.

Manifesto the Great's footman (later known as Mr EX): - a man whose tight trousers stopped traffic.

Footmen : - men from the art centre whose artistic talents were seen as "best utilized serving caffeine" and the like.

Cleaners: - women in apron's, some dreamed of more, others knew the "more" came with a price.

Verruca : - Fanny's daughter, a young woman who proudly wears her name because her mother chose it——— so she was told.

THE DOWNFALL OF MANIFESTO THE GREAT

A Sci-Fi Comedy Where Women Wear Are The Riot Act

PART ONE

In Manifesto the Great's time, there was a huge development of equipment.
He had seen World War I and concluded that bombing things didn't help; instead, he created segregation to control.
"Control is the opposite of chaos," said Manifesto the Great, and some even believed him.

Chapter One

THE ORPHAN

"In the beginning, there was Beryl."–Verruca

*1*935
Beryl was discovered by an elderly reader sitting at the feet of the unfinished statue of her father.

Her mother, a woman with painted nails and love for lying in bed, had passed away moaning about her caffeine not being "hot enough."

Beryl had two choices.

To be swallowed up by the family groomed for a good match or do as her mother suggested and "run away."

She got as far as the courtyard of greatness and realized running away with nowhere to run was a stupid as the headless statue where she now sat.

"Sit at his feet," she'd tell Beryl, usually while Beryl was making her comfortable in bed, "it will lead to things."

Like what? thought Beryl.

She had watched the sun rise, and now it was going down; was she to sleep here?

Clutching her rucksack, she thought of a future with "the family," aunts preening her, telling her what a "no good" her mother was . . .

"Aunts are an earth's invention," her mother used to say, and "you are more him than me."

She wondered if she should go back, take her chances.

She hardly noticed the reader until he stopped.

He looked at the shivering child; her face was familiar, like a colleague he'd worked with years ago in the good old days, when things were easier . . .

She caught his eye.

"My mother told me to wait here," she said.

He looked at her solemn face; she was not even ten.

"At my father's feet," said Beryl.

"Squirt was your father?" said the reader.

Beryl nodded.

"And your mother was that woman?" He whistled through his teeth.

Beryl was one of the last to be born from a man; infertility had ripped through the city like a plague of smallpox, and no one knew why, despite the Librarian pointing to the food chain, but then who listened to the Librarian?

He could see she was special.

She had the intelligent look of her father and the intriguing face of her mother. A heady mixture for an elderly gent who liked intelligent females that were "easy on the eye."

Beryl's father was from the right side of the tracks, who used his head to make profits and mold Beryl's "gullible" mother before she went, well . . . mad.

The reader, a man with no partner and no desire for one, eyed this slip of a girl.

She had potential; he thought maybe even replace that "I have an answer for everything" LM-2, and god knows Manifesto the Great could sure use a new one of her.

Manifesto the Great's ideas were anything but brilliant; in fact, most pissed off the women, sparking "sit-ins" and "sit-outs"—codes for "no bed-diving," which Manifesto the Great in his wisdom blamed on the lack of children; perhaps this Beryl could change things?

If he had known what Beryl's true potential was, he would have sent her to the Art Centre, where children were welcomed, had the freedom to argue, and soon learned it didn't get them anywhere.

But he didn't; instead, he took her back to the Building of Opulence, placed her under the wing of the Librarian, a decision that in the end was the true downfall of Manifesto the Great.

In the ten years of Manifesto the Great's reign, the city had changed into "us and them"; "us" being the readers who ruled and "them" being the rest who bore the brunt of the readers' decisions.

Even though fewer babies were born every year, that less fish swam the rivers, that hills had turned barren, the readers, true "eat drink and be merry" followers, were deaf to any warnings, apart, that is, from the new chairman . . .

There was not even a shellfish to scavenge or a leg to barbecue; flesh-eating had become a luxury and noisy kindergartens a distant memory. All that was left was the odd scraggy four-legged creatures hidden deep in the hills.

Meat was rationed on par with World War II restrictions, sparking off fights over sausages, brawls at barbecues, and demonstrations on par with a four-legged stampede.

The city missed its barbecues and cheese, and, for once, the leaders could do little to help. It wasn't long before hunting and fishing became a distant memory, and meat went underground, illegally stashed under counters and traded in alleyways.

The Librarian, a man not partial to the "eat drink and be merry" philosophy, had warned, but who listened to an elderly man in a wheelchair, especially a man with a passion for wigs? Then when word got out of favors being traded for prawns and giblets, something had to be done.

Manifesto the Great, a positive man, instructed the institute to work on a robust form of fertilization.

The institute came up with growth food, which led to animals large enough to eat within weeks but with flesh toxic with hormones and bland as the Librarian's jokes.

The "new meat," still in its infant stage, was rationed to men under the belief that man's seed was the cure to the whole bugger-all *babies* issue.

Not exactly a popular ruling.

"What about the women?" said the Librarian.

"Let them eat mush," said a voice from the back.

"Here, here," chorused a few.

The Librarian looked at the idiots around the table. "You honestly think a woman is going to eat mush while grilling a chop for her man?"

"Great decisions," said the chairman with an eye on his leader, "are not always greeted with a round of applause."

Chapter Two

THE LIBRARY

"Spying is not an easy thing to do in a wheelchair, no matter how motorized."–The chairman

1930s

When the elderly reader first produced Beryl to the Librarian, he huffed, pointed to a cubby hole of a room, and with a "the sheets are in that cupboard," left her to make herself a bed.

Beryl opened her rucksack. It was pretty empty—a few measly bits of clothing, a dog-eared toothbrush, an old picture of her parents young and hopeful, and her mother's diary.

She hid it under the bed.

"I have a feeling in my waters," said the elderly reader.

"Better head to the loo then."

"Seriously," said the elderly reader.

"So am I," said the Librarian. "The john's the place for that sort of talk."

"There is something about her," said the elderly reader.

"She's a she," said the Librarian. "There is always something about a she, and it's never good."

"She's Squirt's daughter," said the elderly reader.

Silence . . .

Beryl, mid fluffing a pillow, stopped . . .

"That man was a genius with a ledger," said the elderly reader.

"Give him a set of an account and he could make a minus a plus in minutes—seconds even."

The Librarian muttered a "mmm . . ."

"Making money to him was easy," said the elderly reader.

The Librarian nodded. "That's true."

The elderly reader gestured toward the poky room where Beryl was expertly making up a bed, taking in every word.

"She could be the same. The trick is to keep her a secret until we know."

Manifesto the Great, a true leader, continued to ponder; civilization needed children. What was he to do?

He paced the corridors, lost in thought until he caught sight of a cleaner pulling out her mop; then it hit him like a wet flannel.

High on his idea, he raced to the room with a view and burst in to find the readers "studying" an old thirties film on their extra-large mirror perched high on a wall.

"Let's free up the 'fairer sex' for procreation," he proclaimed.

The readers stared at the pint-size leader.

"You been on the caffeine again?" said the chairman.

"Give 'em robots, and they can bed-dive to their hearts' content," smiled Manifesto the Great at his magnificent idea.

"The last thing my 'fairer sex' wants is more time to bed-dive," said a voice from the back.

"Here, here," mumbled a few.

Manifesto the Great, a man of pacing, circled the room, talking of how work and tiredness killed the desire for bed-diving.

"Tell me about it," mumbled a reader.

"Bleach is as off-putting for a woman as, well, false teeth are for . . ." He stopped, stared at the mirror as a voluptuous thirties film star sauntered into view with the sort of comments that went straight to his groin . . .

"Who's that?" he stuttered, watching her disappear.

The Librarian snapped, "You're off your trolley. Women are on the verge of mutiny, and you're talking of bed-diving and earth films?"

"*Pfff*, women," said a few.

"Can't even organize a shopping list, let alone a revolt," said another.

"Too busy with their pots," chuckled another.

Manifesto the Great stared at the mirror. "Does she come back?"

The Librarian fumed; he had a direct view of Fanny's headquarters. He knew all about her "comings and goings." He'd even seen that LM-2 leaving, and he was an expert lip reader.

"The underground hasn't died as everyone believes," he said.

No one listened; he was, after all, a man who could hardly steer his wheelchair, let alone put his wig on straight. What would he know?

Besides, their favorite scene was about to start.

"That Fanny is alive and plotting," said the Librarian.

"Shhhh, she's about to enter," hissed a reader.

"Who?" said Manifesto the Great.

The chairman looked at his leader. "That woman . . . you know."

"Again?" Manifesto the Great's face lit up.

The Librarian eyed the ten men poised about the table, waiting for that woman to appear like she was the second coming.

If that lot thought they could pull the wool over the women's eyes, they were stupider than the whole feed-women-mush idea.

"The women are educating themselves," he said, "grouping together, and they are not going to take mush lying down."

A reader yawned. "No one said anything about lying down."

A few chuckled then stopped as that woman sauntered onto the screen again.

Manifesto the Great sighed; he had never seen anything like her before.

"She's big on earth," said the chairman.

"I can see that," said Manifesto the Great.

"She says what others only dare to think," said a voice from the back.

Manifesto the Great stared at the mirror as Mae West, brandishing a cigarette, eyed her man.

"What's the good of resisting temptation? There will always be more," she said.

Manifesto the Great sighed. "She can hang out my smalls any time."

"Hang out your smalls?" snapped the Librarian. "The women will be hanging out more than that if you don't take some action."

"Why don't you have a nice cup of tea?" said the chairman with a stiff smile at the Librarian.

Chapter Three

JACK AND JOHN

"It is no-nonsense bossing that is the making of a ruler."– Scribed at the feet of a headless statue

few months later . . .
Jack and John were pondering their future in the laundry of the institute, a noisy place where few ventured.

While toying with out-of-date sandwiches, they stared out of the shoebox of a window.

Jack sniffed his milky tea then stirred in sugar while John, pulling gristle from his "meat" sandwich, moaned about the drop in quality.

"You'd never get this on the other side," he said.

"Can't remember the other side; it's so long," said Jack.

He sipped his tea, then pulled a "stewed to buggery" face.

"On the other side was filet meat and crispy rolls," said John.

"*Pfff*, may as well ask for a gold-plated mirror as a crispy roll in this dump," said Jack. "Or a shag."

John choked on his tea.

Jack and John were the only two men from the city who had ventured past the trading post into the outlands, albeit masked and drugged.

Memories of their seed extraction in the shed kept them awake at night. A heady mixture of pain, pleasure, and knock-knock jokes flitted in and out of their dreams like a black-and-white noir thirties film.

At first, they tried to tell of their ordeal but found being laughed at as painful as the thought of seed extraction with no numbing hemp tea. It seemed the Aliens' idea of having any idea of technology was as plausible to the institute as a headless statue receiving flowers.

After all, the Aliens ate with their hands, and they were women—sort of.

Jack peered out the window at the backside of the courtyard of greatness; a mechanical bird flitted onto the headless statue, depositing a watery dropping, followed by a squawk.

Jack watched as the dark fluid slid down the side of the statue's muscular arm. "If only they knew," he sighed.

"Knew what?" said John with a disgusted toss of his sandwich.

The bird jumped out of the way of the bread torpedo.

"The truth about the shed," said Jack.

"We don't know about the truth of the shed," said John.

"We know they took our seed," said Jack.

"Yes, but why?" said John.

Silence . . .

This was the part they always stopped at—the "why."

In the good old days, before they were incarcerated for being "nut jobs," Jack and John had been caretakers of the turtle, in charge of its to-ing and fro-ing.

The turtle collected hormones. For what, they had no idea, let alone how it collected the stuff, but once the turtle escaped under their watch, they had to find, follow, and cover up.

Which was a great plan until kidnapped by the women from the outlands.

The so-called Aliens . . .

Now, years later, John wondered what actually happened and if he knew it could lead to something better, or at least to their old life of decent caffeine and gristle-free sandwiches.

The two watched a mechanical bird leaving more droppings on the headless statue.

They spent several years in the institute answering to such names as "loony" and "fruit loop."

Ignored as losers and useless, they could wander the garden, the corridors, and the kitchen eavesdropping to their hearts' content.

It seemed that women were as discontented as they were.

Manifesto the Great, inspired by *She Done Him Wrong*, a Mae West film that had many a man on the edge of his seat, had come up with the Mae West prototype robot.

The idea of voluptuous mechanical beings bending over, washing baskets while cracking jokes appealed to men, apart from the Librarian, but no one listened to him.

What would a man in a wheelchair and an absurd amount of old fashion wigs know about women?

The women, however, took one look at a robot that could saunter better than they could fluff a cushion and drew up the drawbridge. She hardly inspired "shagging," especially when she made more mess than cleared.

How could any woman worth a soybean "bed-dive" when the robot designed for bed-making made it messier than an orgy?

Bed diving, like fishing, barbecuing, and a good old-fashioned hen-chasing, was off the table.

Men had as much chance of "a good seeing to" as a robot had a day off.

"Do you remember the good old days?" said John.

"Good old days? I can't even remember what I had for breakfast," said Jack. "My memory is as buggered as this so-called tea."

"You say that every time," said John.

"Do I?"

"Yes."

"Well, that's what comes of taking tablets," said Jack.

"We're not on any," said John.

"We're not?" said Jack.

"No," said John.

"Maybe we should be," laughed Jack.

Chapter Four

AGGIE

"The handing over of things has nothing to do with hands."– Aggie

Manifesto the Great stared into the dark. He couldn't see a thing except for a few flecks of light through the porous hemp sack shoved over his head.

He huffed, inhaling the hemp fumes, and stumbled.

Tork grabbed his arm, ignoring Maisie's "typical" look.

"Must we go through this every time?" said Manifesto the Great.

"Imperative," said Maisie with a rough, steading gesture about his back.

"I am the leader, you know," said Manifesto the Great.

"Only in the city," snapped Tork.

Manifesto the Great stumbled on.

"I liked it better when she snuck into the city," he muttered.

"Yeah, well, that's not gonna happen, is it?" snapped Tork.

"Pulling the hemp over that Librarian's eyes always tickled me."

"Hardly a reason to move her, is it?" said Tork.

"I know," he sighed.

Manifesto the Great shuffled his feet along the rocky path; the terrain had changed, a new path, just as he had familiarized himself with the old one. It was all part of their so-called "keep him in the dark" tactics.

"I could get Manifesto the Great's footman to transport her," said Manifesto the Great. "Some of them are excellent drivers."

"A transporter out here?" Maisie snorted a jeer.

"Why not?" said Manifesto the Great.

He stumbled again . . .

"Shit!"

Tork made as if to grab the leader and missed as Manifesto the Great tripped, crashing to his knees with a loud "son of sperm."

"Mind," said Tork.

"Bit late for that," snapped Manifesto the Great.

Tork and Maisie pulled him to his feet and waited as he brushed himself off.

"A transport out here is as useful as a bee in a shed," said Maisie.

"Very poignant," said Manifesto the Great with an exaggerated knee rub.

"A bird in a bucket," said Maisie.

"I get the picture," he huffed.

"May as well put a jar over its head and let it suffocate," said Maisie.

"I said I get it!" snapped the leader. "Just because I've got a bag over my head doesn't mean my brain's hibernating."

"I mean, what good is a transport with no roads?" said Maisie.

The leader stood to attention. "I know that!"

He stopped. "I could get the jack-of-all-trades to—you know, build a road."

"All they do is strike," snapped Tork.

"And blabber," said Maisie, "like that friggin' footman."

"Yes, well, I sorted that, didn't I?" said Manifesto the Great.

"Sorted it? It took three footmen raids and several settler attacks before you sorted it. We've had to move camp more times than the Librarian changes his wigs."

Manifesto the Great said nothing.

The last footman to accompany Manifesto the Great blabbed big-time, which led to several midnight raids, depleting the Alien's farm stock and the Aliens resettling.

"We're in the middle of nowhere thanks to your so-called civilized men," said Maisie.

"Okay, so they were a little zealous," huffed Manifesto the Great.

"Zealous? If they knew where we lived, our colony would be buggered."

Manifesto the Great sighed. He hated it when Tork was right, let alone Maisie; she could really rub it in.

Manifesto the Great continued to walk; the ground changed from rocky to sand, he was nearly there . . .

He stumbled on hearing the crackle of the campfire, the muttering of the Aliens; then, he heard a familiar cough.

His foot fumbled over a rock, his leg crashed into a log seat, and before he found his balance, Tork pushed him into a seat as Maisie, like a magician revealing a rabbit, pulled his head bag off.

The leader wiped the sweat from his face and breathed in the fresh air.

His eyes adjusted to the firelight as he caught the fiery eyes of an elderly woman with sun-bleached skin and hair down her back.

For a moment, he smiled; the cloak-and-dagger journey—the skinned knees forgotten.

"Mother," he whispered.

Her eyes fluttered open.

His face softened.

Over the years, Manifesto the Great had come to appreciate his mother, despite their differences of opinion. She was a haven of rationality, a retreat from the readers and their stupid ideas, and he wanted to savor every moment.

The readers, poised for their morning meeting in the room with a view, watched the chairman prepare his notes.

He looked up and sighed.

"How long before that bozo arrives?" he snapped.

The readers shifted uncomfortably.

"How long is a piece of pulling rope?" a reader laughed nervously.

An oaf-like footman coughed. "He is saying goodbye, sir."

"Saying goodbye to what?" said the chairman. "His virginity?"

"No, sir, it's a family thing," said the oaf-like footman.

The readers threw Manifesto the Great's footman a "shut it" look.

"A family thing? What is he, a character in a Victorian melodrama?" said the chairman.

"Sir, melodramas are as out-of-date as flappers; it's musicals now watched." The oaf-like footman paused with a questioning raised eyebrow. "Mae West?"

"So, you're telling me our leader is in a musical?" said the chairman.

"No, sir, he is saying goodbye to his mother," said the oaf of a footman.

The chairman spat out his caffeine.

The readers said nothing.

"Did you know about this?" he choked.

The readers nodded.

"We have a meat black market running rife, butchers under attack paying protection money, and our leader is saying goodbye to our enemy?" He eyeballed the committee with his best glare. "Did you not think to tell me?"

"He said not to," said a small a voice from the back.

The chairman flashed him a look.

"They are hardly enemies, sir; they are the field workers. We'd be lost without them," said the oaf-like footman.

The chairman huffed. "But they haven't solved the four-legged problem, have they?"

Silence.

"Our leader is in the outer lands." The chairman shook his head. "He could be kidnapped."

"And would that be such a bad thing?" said the small voice.

The chairman stopped. *Is that Manifesto the Great's footman?*

He looked at his comrades.

They waited.

"Well, I guess not," he muttered.

Aggie snuggled into her blanket.

"Before you say anything, I'm not coming back with you. I don't want to die in that city."

She stopped to catch her breath.

"This is my home."

She gasped for air.

Tork placed an inhaler cone over her nose; she breathed in the hemp fumes.

The leader waited.

Her eyes softened in a "thank you" look at Tork.

Tork removed the inhaler cone.

Aggie looked at her son.

"What have you been eating?"

"Just the usual," said the leader.

"You look puffy, smell a bit . . . off," said Aggie.

Manifesto the Great sniffed his armpits. "Do I?"

"You've been overdoing the meat again, haven't you?"

"It's the new breed of hens," said the leader. "Ten days, and they're ready to roast."

"You're roasting birds now?" she coughed.

"Well, yes, we have to roast something."

Tork offered the inhaler; she brushed her aside.

"I can bring you one," said Manifesto the Great. "They fatten up like a balloon. There's so much flesh they can hardly walk."

"What's wrong with a potato?" said Aggie.

"It's hardly juicy," said the leader.

"Juice's more important than the survival of the planet?" said Aggie.

"I do my best to eat the odd nuts, but I need real flesh to think and lead the city."

She mumbled something about Cat's ability to think on seeds and stopped.

"All that flesh is not good for you," she said. "Especially if you're feeding them 'stuff.'"

"It's not stuff; it's hormones," said the leader.

"Hormones? We Aliens never needed any of that stuff."

"But we're not eating you, are we?"

"And what about Fanny, then? Have you made your peace?" Aggie started to cough again.

"Well, sort of. To be honest, I thought the robots might help, stop the whole women's we-want-more thing."

"*Pfff*," said Maisie.

Manifesto the Great looked at Tork. "Isn't it what all women want? More time for bed-diving?"

Tork said nothing; she couldn't remember the last time she'd bed-dived. The closest she got was washing Aggie's back.

"You can't offer robots to a woman and expect her to give up a good night's sleep," said Maisie.

"I don't hear any complaints," lied Manifesto the Great. "And they do everything a woman can."

His mother threw him a "really" cough.

"Well, almost everything," mumbled the leader.

Chapter Five

THE SPEECH

"Spying is easy in a wheelchair; no one sees you."–The Librarian

Manifesto the Great stared out of the grand balcony, his tiny frame barely reaching the top of the ledge.

He could hear the readers behind him arguing in the newly refurbished, enlarged-to-the-height-of-luxury room with a view.

The load of bollocks room.

Every day the readers sat around the extra-large table arguing like they knew what they were talking about, while footmen stood to attention in the corners poised for beverage requirements.

With a sigh, he stared into the sky.

Manifesto the Great's footman slid the "viewing box" by the leader's feet. Manifesto the Great ignored it; what did he care of a view when his mum was dying?

How was he to rule without her?

The readers were useless; their answer to the lack of babies and shagging was a breeding policy that had Manifesto the Great choking on his tea.

How do they control the masses with that?

"There'll be riots," he said.

The readers laughed; it never occurred to them that they could not control the masses, despite Manifesto the Great's doomed "free up the fairer sex for more bed-diving" initiative.

"We need to separate women into those with potential and those of the herding variety," shouted the chairman.

"Here, here," echoed the other readers.

Manifesto the Great sighed.

The real birds had flown south decades ago; how he missed them.

"Women with potential to produce babies," shouted the chairman.

"Here, here," said the readers.

The Librarian's wheelchair crashed through the door, followed by his wizened frame covered in blankets and a dusty Marie Antoinette wig poised on his head.

Some called him a "Dandy," which the Librarian chose to ignore, just because he loved wigs. The truth was, he lost his hair at fifteen.

"Potential? From a woman?" he shouted. "You have no idea of their potential, even if it slapped you in the face."

The readers didn't react, let alone look.

They had seen it all before. He was always bursting in, despite being "put out to pastures" years ago.

"And with the longevity gene," said the chairman.

"Longevity gene? You'll regret that," sneered the Librarian.

"As for the herding variety"—the chairman eyed his comrades—"we'll be assigning them to gardening and cleaning duties."

"Assigned? Since when do we assign women?" said the Librarian.

The chairman looked at the Librarian like he was an ant.

"Needs must in these hard times," said the chairman.

"Needs must?" said the Librarian, circling the room. "Bit late for that, isn't it?"

"It's never too late," laughed a voice from the back.

"You've got as much chance of controlling the masses with that stupid idea as Manifesto the Great here has of doing the high jump." He shouted to Manifesto the Great, "What do you think of this 'needs must' malarky?"

"Leave him," said a voice from the back.

"His mother," he mouthed.

The others mumbled to each other.

"Yes, yes."

"Sad state of affairs."

"Sad?" snapped the Librarian. "That woman was the bane of my life."

The chairman, with a "here we go" face, snapped, "Bane? She must be ninety at least."

"Exactly," shouted the Librarian, pulling a robust wheelie. "'Bout time she kicked the bucket."

A sharp intake of breath filled the room. The readers turned to Manifesto the Great's back. Did he hear?

Manifesto the Great didn't even twitch; he had stopped listening to the Librarian years ago.

"Manifesto!" shouted the Librarian.

Silence—not a move.

The Librarian headed out to the balcony. "Come back in here and take command, or this lot will be making more decisions like those Mae West robots."

John and Jack stared out of their window, watching an extra-large turtle stand by the back of the institute for what seemed an eternity.

Giant turtles were a nuisance in the city, stumbling into gardens and holding up traffic, now and then herded away by the foreigners into the outlands.

They were invented to fetch and carry hormones at first, but soon, it was anything.

"What I wouldn't give to be taken seriously," said John.

"And drink decent tea," sighed Jack.

"Something different to happen," said John.

"Try losing your memory," sighed Jack. "Every chore is new."

The turtle shuffled into action, making its way to the garden for a good old sniff at the roses, the cleaner's prized possessions.

"Here we go," muttered John.

Jack began to *hmmm*.

"Wonder why he comes here," said John.

Jack shrugged. "Maybe he is a she,"

"It's a robot," said John.

"Looking for sandwiches," said Jack, hurling the last of his at the turtle.

The turtle jumped out of the way.

Jack, with a laugh, emptied his tea out the window, missing the turtle by inches.

"Will you stop with the hurling?" hissed John.

Jack, grabbing John's sandwich remains, hit the turtle with perfect aim.

The turtle glared up at the window.

"Now look what you've done."

"It's an omen," said Jack.

John threw him a look.

"I have a weird feeling down below," said Jack.

"*Pfff*, you and your feelings. What you need is some good evacuation water."

Jack didn't answer; evacuation water was John's answer to everything.

The *Greenhouse Manual* slid from Aggie's hand as Tork helped her to bed.

Aggie grasped Tork's hand with a firm grip and then closed her eyes and let go.

Tork covered her with a blanket.

Aggie's last place of rest was in Tork's hut, where they first lived, laughed, and argued together.

As Tork made her comfortable, Aggie's life paraded before her eyes. She smiled as she thought of Tork and their times in the fields together, their picnics, Tork's hands sliding to hidden places performing things that only she and the odd ants knew.

They called it "field-bashing," "midday brunch," and "waiting for the tea to boil," but never "shagging."

Aggie looked into Tork's eyes and touched her tears.

"You're still young," she whispered. "You'll find someone else."

Tork kissed her finger.

She loved her life with Aggie. They had shared the same dream and built it together.

Thanks to Jack and John's seeds, procreation in a Petri dish took off, and baby-making in the shed became as easy as whipping up home brew, which, in the end, divided the Alien community in two:

Those who loved babies and those that wanted a good night's sleep.

Those that loved them set up the hippie colony with Tork and Aggie, where the babies were nurtured and wind and water energy was discovered.

While those who preferred animals became field workers living in their old huts with Cat, the place where the first batch of teenagers was sent to "cut their teeth."

No one ever thought about Jack and John, despite several look-alikes, as the embryos never produced a male baby.

Apart from, that is, Aggie.

"They'll be back," she often said. "Their memories will sharpen."

The Aliens laughed their heads off.

Jack and John back? As if? They couldn't even find their way out of a hemp bag, let alone pass the black hills.

Aggie was not convinced.

Tork helped Aggie to sit up. Tork wiped her lips and offered her tea for pain.

Aggie coughed.

The hippies and field workers had congregated outside in hushed reverence.

"Read the last page to me," she said to Tork.

"Now?" said Tork. "Your son will be here soon."

"I want to hear one more time."

She coughed again.

A few of the field workers pushed the windows open and peered in.

"That's what you said last time," said Tork with a soft look.

She spluttered into her tea, gesturing a "carry on" as Manifesto the Great arrived, silently parting the crowd like it was the Red Sea.

He pushed through the door, leaving it ajar.

The hippies peered through as Manifesto the Great caught Tork's eye.

"She wants me to read," said Tork.

Manifesto the Great didn't even hear; all he could see was the life draining from his mother's face.

Tork opened the *Guide*; a hush fell on the group as she began to read.

The Ramblings of a Dying Woman.
I love my body, from the deliciously farting bowels to the breast that gave me pleasure. It has devoured food so delicious I drool, to bed-diving so spectacular my pelvis lubricates at the thought and a heart that loved so much that it ached.

A few sighed. *So poetic.*

My body has been there for me through thick and thin. Crying when I needed to, dancing until it dropped, and laughing with gusto, turning a bleak day into a comedy sketch.
Even frail and old, wheeled about in a chair, my body has not let me down. With gums that fill with juices at the mere smell of sweet hemp, to full thick hair that delights in the stroking of my lover.

Tork looked at her partner.

I love my body and those I shared it with.

I give in to its passing with gratitude and thank the gods of the galaxies for designing such a miraculous and efficient machine to live in and another to share it with.

"Mum," said Manifesto the Great; he clutched her hand as Aggie spat out a hemp tablet and gasped her last breath.

Chapter Six

GRISTLE

"Never judge a sandwich by its crust."–Jack

Several days later, John, clutching a recycling bag under the veranda, watched the cleaner exit under a volley of swear words.

The garden was full of uneaten sandwiches hurled by Jack, hell-bent on, as he put it, "leaving a trail for the gods of the galaxy."

The head cleaner took one look at the now "trash heap of a garden" and, with a brisk shove of her broom, ordered the men to "clean it up."

John had tried to warn Jack.

"The gods of the galaxy don't do bread," he said, not that Jack listened.

With a long sigh, John stared at the afternoon sky; any minute, the sun would burst from the clouds, sending anyone under it into a pool of sweat.

Jack hummed.

"Must you always lob things?" said John.

"It's what a window is for," said Jack.

"I thought that was what bins were for."

Jack shrugged. "Bins mean nothing to me; my memory's buggered."

"So you say," snapped John.

"Besides, I have a feeling in my waters," said Jack.

"*Pfff*," huffed John.

The two men stared into the garden, each waiting for the other to "pick up," when a Mae West robot sauntered into view.

John stared at the rope trailing behind her like a stripper's whip and sighed. "Now we have to wait till this berk of a robot gets its washing line act together."

"I know," chuckled Jack.

"It'll take forever," said John.

"Best part," said Jack.

John threw him a look. "Thought you said your memory was buggered?"

The Mae West robot wrapped the rope around a tree, then turned to find another.

"It's an omen," said Jack.

"It's a robot," said John.

"Things are afloat." Jack gestured "down below." "I can feel it."

"Yeah, right," muttered John.

Jack nodded toward a crust curling in the sun. "That is there for a reason."

"You tossed it," snapped John.

"For a reason," said Jack.

The Mae West robot tried to attach her rope to a veranda pole that was way too short. She untied the rope and sashayed back indoors, trailing the rope behind her.

"Get out," shouted the cleaner.

The Mae West robot reappeared without the rope.

The rope sailed through the air like a cricket ball crashlanding on the robot's forehead. It flopped to her feet.

"And tie that thing before you lose it!" shouted the cleaner.

With a nonchalant swish of her blonde wig, the Mae West robot picked it up and strutted back to the tree.

"Told you. An omen," said Jack.

"Hardly an omen," huffed John, "more like a repeat performance."

He looked about. "Where did that turtle go?"

Jack shrugged.

"You can never trust an out-of-sight turtle."

Jack said nothing.

"There are rumors of Aliens hiding in turtles."

"Rumors are nothing compared to what I feel down below," said Jack.

With a look that could dose a fire, John was about to tell Jack where he could shove his feelings when the turtle's head peered from the top of a hedge like a spy.

It blinked.

John watched as it came into view, sniffing about the pseudo pansies, an innovation to discourage real flower-sniffing.

"There's something different about that turtle," said John.

The turtle sniffed the pansy.

"Here we go," sighed Jack.

"I thought you said—" John stopped and caught a look in Jack's soft eyes. "Never mind."

The turtle sniffed again, then, with a disappointed roar, stamped the offending flower, following with another roar.

The turtle spit sprayed forth onto Mae West, sparking off an electrical storm in her thought processes.

"Come up and . . . come up and . . . see mmm-me . . . mmm-me," she circled mechanically.

The turtle roared, raining spit like a fire hose.

Mae West, now fuzzed up to the eyeballs, circled faster.

"Is th-th-th-that a g-g-g-gun . . . is that a g-g-g-gun . . . or you just . . . p-p-p-please . . ."

The cleaner appeared, brandishing a broom like Damocles's sword.

Tork built a huge fire for Aggie. Maisie collected the drums while the shover, now old and grey with little movement left in her legs, perched by the fire, painting the teenager's bodies.

The teenagers had their ideas of saying goodbye, dancing with painted bodies being one of them, which had some elders tutting.

The hippies and field workers disagreed on many things; in fact, arguing was as frequent to them as making a brew, and brewing up was continuous. There was always a kettle bubbling like a witch's cauldron somewhere.

Working in the fields did it.

So many trees had been cut that the once-lush hills were black and barren with a biting wind that whipped about the fields. Drinking tea kept the workers warm until the sun came out.

An afternoon sun so hot that it burned backs and faces, parching a throat so dry that only a sip of cooled sweet tea could cure.

The ceremony of death, like tea, however, was something both hippies and fieldworkers agreed on.

The burning ceremony took place in silence, while the scattering of ashes required a quiet ceremony of words and song.

The ashes were always scattered about the shed—the place of birth for many, apart from Cat, who came from a spaceship, planet unknown.

Cat was the last from the spaceship to die, the last of the ashes to fly across the shiny surfaces of said spaceship and cling for days. In fact, the clinging of her ashes was something of a record, glued for weeks despite the strong winds.

Some say it was her last hoorah, her last stab of control; others claimed it was revenge.

Cat wanted her hut, and all in it burned. However, the field workers rummaged, claiming that Cat was a contrary sort who wanted not only "rummaging" but also a spot of "memento-keeping."

The truth was, there were diaries hidden in her hut, *Life by the Dashboard* being the most notable. A diary with an extensive chapter on "the John," a toilet unused but filled with the "logs" of earlier years.

After the scattering of ashes, the field workers and hippies gathered around the campfire. With hemp-induced reminisces, they roasted vegetables and joked about what they had learned from the dead and what was so annoying about her.

Cat's roasting took so many nights that it was declared a holiday.

Chapter Seven

THE TURTLE

"Never judge a rope by its length."–The unknown cleaner

Jack and John were inside a turtle, and not even the cleaner had a clue.

It's not like they had planned it; it just sort of happened.

It was the rope, the cleaner's broom.

"Grab it!" She yelled as if her life depended on it while chasing the turtle with her broom.

The two men watched, wondering just what the cleaner thought a broom could do to a turtle large enough to sit on without seeing the ground.

Anyone would think the rope was made of gold the way the cleaner yelled. Six months of disappearing rope could do that to a cleaner—or *Bette*, as she liked to call herself (she had a fondness for Bette Davis's films).

She was fed up replacing a washing line out of her own pocket and fed up dealing with the sort of robot that turned mundane duties into a war zone, and she was damn well not buying another rope.

An expert at throwing a Bette Davis look that could propel even the most comatose of men into action, Bette ruled the institute services department. She could wield a broom like a sword, a mop like a lightsaber, even when wet, and as for a bucket?

In Bette's hands, a bucket was a weapon of mass destruction that she threw with the force of a shotput and the aim of a dart's champion.

Ducking was never quick enough.

Bette, with a "make yourself useful" scream, hurled her bucket at John when the turtle disappeared out of the gate with the rope trailing behind.

John, mid ducking, saw an opportunity—an opportunity he grabbed along with Jack.

They followed the seemingly "gold-plated" rope out of the garden, into the street, past the institute's secret entrance and its camouflaged door.

John looked at Jack. *It usually stopped there,* he thought.

Jack hummed.

They followed as it passed the backside of the courtyard of greatness and into the back alleys of Main Street.

Where the hell was it going? thought John.

Jack, his head as empty as a dead battery, continued to hum.

The turtle, mid trot, stopped.

A sharp whistle came from above.

John pulled Jack behind a garbage bin.

Jack pulled a face made to cough, and John clasped his hand over his mouth with a "shhhh."

He watched as Fanny, dressed in bright red and heels, climbed down a drainpipe followed by the Poet, the Warden, LM-2, the Beverage Maker, and the Sidekick, all in various shades of red.

"Where's the funeral?" whispered Jack.

"I don't know, but we're gonna find out," hissed John, his intuition working overtime.

This could be the following of a lifetime, thought John. *The trailing that could turn things.*

As the last of the heeled feet disappeared inside the turtle, John, holding his breath, and Jack grabbed the rope and pulled. The two men landed into the sort of crevice that only a masked sewage worker would enter.

Jack's humming abruptly stopped as he began to swear on par with a porn star until John threatened to place his now-dirty hand on his mouth.

"This puts our friendship in a whole new light," hissed Jack, latching on to something he'd rather not see.

John did too. "What the devil do these things eat?" was on the tip of his tongue, when Jack passed out.

Once out of the city, the women climbed astride the turtle-like rodeo riders while Jack and John climbed inside the much-cleaner "looting and carrying things cavity" and began a futile brushing down.

"This could be the making of us," said John, trying to convince himself.

Jack, inhaling the filtered air, scowled; he was covered in shit.

The washerwoman was making a stew, which, to be frank, was nothing to get excited about. Now an elderly woman with senses not worth a jot and little to work with plant-wise, her stew was about as tasty as a vitamin pill. Still, she did her best; it was, after all, Aggie's roasting. She deserved at least a stew worth a second helping.

She turned to the bin-emptier, sniffing while scraping the last of the washerwoman's peelings. "Get a grip," she was about to shout when the turtle jolted to a halt, juddering Fanny almost off her back.

"You'll find 'em at the shed," she shouted.

John and Jack looked at each other; could it be the same shed?

They watched through the gap of the turtle's leg joint as the turtle took them through the scenic route of the camp.

Past the teenagers practicing their song "Ode to Aggie," past the large bonfire, the rows of huts, the vegetable patches, and several hemp-chewing four-legged creatures until they arrived at the shed with Tork reverently clutching an urn.

The shed, thanks to the ashes of many, was a place of scented, larger-than-life flowers. The two men almost passed out with the heady perfume until the singing started, off-key like a squawking flock of crows.

The men covered their ears.

The singing was followed with poetry, chanting, and, finally, the scattering of ashes, which involved working out which way the wind blew with the licking of a finger.

John was impressed; not many did that in the city. Ashes were scattered with no thought of the wind. Some even laughed when the ashes blew back.

Not here; there was a quiet reverence as Tork held her finger to the wind, followed by a serene repositioning and a "to you, Aggie" chant.

Aggie's ashes sailed across the horizon like a distant bird formation.

John almost felt something.

Jack wiped a tear, claiming it to be an itch.

Tork was quiet as the women made their way to the bonfire. She hardly noticed the teenagers' dance, the bin emptier lighting the fire, or the spread of roasted vegetables nearby.

She was in a grieving trance.

She slumped onto a log, her heavy heart so broken she couldn't even face a hemp tea, let alone muster a story for the roasting.

She stared at the fire while the washerwomen began reminiscing of Aggie's first sighting of a rat.

"She screamed," laughed a voice from the back.

"Like a banshee," chuckled another.

Tork closed her eyes. What she'd give to hear that scream just one more time.

Fanny sat beside her, bristling with plans. There were rumors that she had lost it; even a dying Aggie wondered about her sanity.

It was the Mae West robots that had pushed her to the edge. Now installed in most "comfortable" homes, women had little to do but churn out the odd baby and entertain men in the bedroom.

The Mae West robots did everything else, and what made it worse was the fear of no baby. She had even heard of barren women being made homeless.

"We're supposed to not only lie down and think of Planet Hy Man but do it with leather, whips, and jokes," said Fanny. "And produce into the bargain."

Tork tossed a twig at the fire.

"Whip?" said the Poet, passing a mug of hemp to Tork. "Is that not for climbing trees?"

Tork looked up. "There are many uses for leather." She almost smiled at the memory.

"Whip?" said Fanny. "I'll give 'em something to whip about. My underwire is poised and ready."

Tork's face softened. Aggie used to laugh at Fanny's "weapons of mass destruction" rants; it was one of their private jokes.

"Tork doesn't want to hear about liberating women just now," said the Poet. She slid a comrade arm around Tork. "She's grieving."

Fanny, ignoring the Poet, nudged Tork. "I have a plan," she said. "It will make Aggie proud."

Chapter Eight

ASHES TO ASHES

"Talking with eyes is the beginning of love."–Tork

Manifesto the Great and LM-2 watched the scattering of ashes from a distance. LM-2 looked at the leader, his small frame shrunk with grief.

Grief was something she barely remembered, her heart having toughened over the years like the callus of an old foot.

LM-2 went underground the day she decided that Aliens were not for her.

Hell-bent on an existence that gave women some sort of choice, even if it was just coffee, she was devoted to Fanny's vision, despite Fanny being the most annoying woman on the planet.

Fanny had rigged up the basement of her husband's office as the underground headquarters where LM-2 spent her time making leaflets and trying to persuade Fanny that there was nothing more to a bra than underwire.

She had her work cut out for her.

"Remember those days of shell collecting?" he said.

LM-2 said nothing; she hated those days.

Manifesto the Great kicked a stone. "Best days of my life," he said.

LM-2 didn't answer.

"It's rubbish being a leader."

He kicked another stone.

"I mean, everyone thinks it's great—the bees' knees. Well, they should try keeping that rabble of bozos in line for a while."

LM-2 eyed him; she had no time for self-pity.

"And do the punters appreciate it?"

"If you want me to feel sorry for you, you can forget it," said LM-2. "You got what you deserved."

"Me?"

"Yes," said LM-2. "All you men are alike."

Manifesto the Great grabbed another stone and tossed it with venom. "I'm not like my father."

"The only difference between him and you is your height and, well, the other thing."

Manifesto the Great blushed; everyone expected him to be putting it about like his father. The only thing he put about was his opinion. His pecker was tucked away, and as far as he was concerned, it was staying that way. He had as much interest in shagging as LM-2 did in his moaning.

Manifesto the Great thought of his grandfather's statue; he thought he emulated him more than his stupid father.

"I'm not going back with you," she said.

"Never asked."

"Yes, but you thought it."

"Actually," he said, "I need eyes, ears, and, well, reporting."

"You mean spying."

"Well, not exactly spying . . . more keeping me in the loop."

He tossed another stone.

"I think they are plotting against me."

"Who?" said LM-2.

"The readers."

"*Pfff*, them; they couldn't plot a novel, let alone a coup."

"They follow the chairman, and he's a dangerous man."

"I thought the Librarian was the dangerous one?"

"Him?" said Manifesto the Great. "All he's good for these days is brushing his wigs, and they're as out-of-date as a spaceship."

She looked at him, and they both laughed.

Maisie and Fanny watched the sunset over the burning on the lake.

The flames flickered reflections in the mirror like water as the full moon rose. A bat fluttered by; Fanny jumped.

Maisie stretched out her hand.

Fanny grasped it.

"Thank you," said Fanny.

Fanny smiled at her, then looked back at the full moon; it had been a long time.

The moon always looked better on the fields—larger, more dominating—and tonight, on a clear sky, it was the best Fanny had seen in a long time. As the couple watched the Milky Way flicker into view, Maisie again thanked Fanny.

"You didn't have to stay," she said.

"But I wanted to," said Fanny.

Maisie, a woman with the strength of a bear, had wrestled four-legged creatures many times, but she was useless when Aggie died, overcome with grief.

Fanny slid her arm around Maisie and was about to reassure her it was "okay to cry" when another bat flapped millimeters from Fanny's cheek.

She squealed.

Maisie laughed.

Maisie had ridden the turtle many times with Fanny, Maisie at the front and Fanny behind with her arms around Maisie's waist and the wind in her hair. In fact, Fanny always pulled her hair out when mounting a turtle, just for that purpose. The wind made her feel free, and being pressed against the power of Maisie's body was an experience she had never felt before.

Maisie had the muscles of a wrestler; in fact, she was one. She wrestled every day with anyone who looked at her sideways—apart from, that is, Fanny.

Over the ten years of Manifesto the Great's rule, Fanny and Maisie rode the turtle, back and forth, full of instruments, equipment, and books for the hippie colony.

Aggie was an excellent list-maker, Fanny was a marvel at sourcing, and the turtle was putty in Maisie's hands.

Packing the insides of a turtle at the dead of night, her man comatose with a belly full of meat, was Fanny's favorite time. After feeding her owner with enough flesh to feed a football team, she'd sneak out, meet her lover, and together, clutching Aggie's mile-long list, they'd pillage, pilfer, laugh, and whisper.

Fanny had never laughed so much.

Pilfering in silence took the whole adventure to a new level, and Fanny often felt like a hysterical schoolgirl. Stifling a giggle with Maisie was the most fun she'd ever had—apart from, that is, sleeping with her.

Fanny's life was one long, secret adventure until there were no more lists, and the turtle was spent like an old rifle cartridge.

"We're all good," said Aggie, packing the last of the Bunsen burners into the shed.

"Oh," said Fanny. She looked at Maisie. "No more pilfering needed then?"

Aggie shook her head as the turtle, its mechanical joints worn threadbare, made its way to the tree and slumped to the ground.

"Just as well," said Aggie. "That turtle is done, ready for the big sleep under the tree."

"There are plenty more turtles," muttered Fanny.

The turtle, with a half-hearted groan, nestled against the tree trunk.

"So, what do you need now?" said Fanny.

"Nothing," said Aggie.

"Oh, but what will I tell my underground?" said Fanny.

Aggie looked from Fanny to Maisie. "There is always a place for you here," she said, knowing, like Maisie, that Fanny would never move.

Fanny had her underground, office, and women to save; there was so much to do.

She shook her head. Sure, riding with Maisie over the fields was an adventure, but like LM-2, she did not want to spend the rest of her life using water from a bucket or eating with her hands. A bonfire was fun, but Fanny liked a tablecloth, the smell of ironed linen, hot water, and soft towels more.

She looked at Maisie. "You could come," she said, knowing full well the last place Maisie would want to be was in the city.

Maisie liked the smell of smoke, skin brushing with a wire brush, and soap that didn't lather. The only sort of linen she knew was toilet paper.

She gagged at the thought of soft towels. She wanted salt scrubs and an arm wrestling, and the chances of that in the city were as likely as a mechanical turtle churning out milk.

Besides, Maisie had no time for underwire.

"Making a weapon out of that," said Maisie, "was as laughable as silent pilfering."

Chapter Nine

THE SHED

"The scent of the past jump-starts a memory better than any photo."–Jack

It was dark when the two men jumped from the turtle. The shed was easy to enter: just a jiggle with a twig and the lock fell open like a cracked nut. John paused and looked at Jack as distant laughter filled the air.

"Should we?" he said.

Jack, without a backward glance, pushed his way through. It was all coming back to him—that time in the shed.

He stopped at the entrance and stared.

The room was the same but enlarged, with way more mini-bars, all making that familiar humming sound he remembered so well.

The walls were covered with shelves, Petri dishes, and test tubes, the counter with Bunsen burners, gloves, and a selection of instruments sparking more memories for Jack.

At the back of the shed, the women had added a conservatory with a tree sprouting through a skylight and jars of small glistening balls swinging from the branches.

"The shed looks so small from the outside," said John.

"That's science for you," said Jack. He lifted a test tube, jiggled it, and sniffed; the smell was familiar.

John fingered a white coat on the back of a chair. "There's nothing backward about these women," he said.

Jack lifted another test tube and sniffed. "Definitely."

"I mean, how did they get that tree to do that?" said John.

"Unfathomable."

John turned to his friend. "You okay, mate?"

Jack nodded.

"It's just that you look . . . different," said John.

"Never felt better."

"Like the lights are back on?" said John.

"They certainly are," said Jack.

John opened a fridge.

"I can remember everything," said Jack.

John poked about. "That's good."

"I know what these are for," said Jack, gesturing to a Petri dish.

"Great," said John; he moved to the back of the shed.

"And this," said Jack, lifting a Bunsen burner.

"Hmm, so you said."

"It's for destabilizing," said Jack.

"Exactly," said John.

Jack followed. "But not as we know it."

John stopped at the tree and looked up at the branches stretching into the sky. "White coat wearers are always destabilizing."

"Yes, but this is for something different," said Jack.

John flicked a ball with his finger; it glistened.

"Wonder what these are for?"

"They're making babies," said Jack.

"Aye, very good," muttered John.

"And those, my friend, are balls," said Jack.

"I can see that," said John.

"Your balls," said Jack.

John dropped his hand.

"Or mine. Synthesized by the look of it."

John looked at his fingers in disbelief.

"These women are making babies," said Jack.

"Babies? In a shed?"

"With test tubes," said Jack.

"Test tubes? From a woman?" said John.

Jack nodded. "Petri dishes, too."

"It's not possible," said John.

"Loads, by the look," said Jack.

"The institute had talked of such things," said John, "but . . ."

He stared at the Petri dishes; this could be their chance to make it back to the other side. No more "fruit loop" calling, maybe even their names on statues.

"Kismet has brought us here," said John. "Fate, the gods of the galaxies. This is our destiny."

"We should leave," said Jack.

"Leave?" said John. "We should take some of this back."

"Don't think we should," said Jack.

"I mean, if this is what women can do, imagine what we can," said John.

"Not a good idea, mate," said Jack.

"Just think, we could be back on the other side—gristle-free sandwiches by the plateful." John slapped Jack's shoulder. "Pâté and filet."

Jack shook his head.

"The old Jack and John, back in white coats," laughed John with another slap.

Jack whistled through his teeth. "I still don't think it is a good idea."

"Yes, but it's ages since you thought," said John, grabbing a bag.

"But the women in the city with no babies. What will they do when they find out about all this?"

John stopped and looked at his pal. "There was a time when you wouldn't even have asked that question."

Chapter Ten

THE OAF OF A FOOTMAN

"A woman with time on her hands is a revolution waiting to happen."–The Librarian

Manifesto the Great stared at his meatloaf.

Normally he would have wondered about a cocktail, something "Mae West like," maybe even eat his meatloaf in front of one of her films, but not now.

Since his mother died, he had not even removed the cover from his mirror, let alone left his room.

His grief was a deep emptiness that overwhelmed him and held him prisoner.

He poked his meatloaf, not even noticing the cheese bubbling on the top.

His relationship with his mother had been fraught with many feelings. There were words he regretted, huffs he wished he could take back, and as he had no offspring, he had no idea the depth of forgiveness a parent could feel.

His footman, a kind man from settler stock, felt sorry for his leader.

He, too, had lost a parent: his father, on a hunt which involved a trek across the black hills for the elusive four-legged creature with thighs so large they took days to cook.

James the Strong had seen such a barbecue in the mirror, a goat stuffed and buried in the ground taking days to cook and leading to the tastiest of meats.

Why not a four-legged creature, the sort that roamed the distant hills that legends were made of?

The footmen drew straws as to who would follow; his father lost and was never seen again, apart from a half-eaten sock.

Not long after Manifesto the Great's footman's disappearance, the do-not-open gate was erected, and hunting was never mentioned again.

Manifesto the Great's footman gestured to the meatloaf. "Tuck in," he said. "You'll feel better."

Manifesto the Great looked at the slim footman.

He had never noticed him before, but his concern soothed him.

"If only I had another five minutes," he muttered. "To tell her that I didn't mean the things I said, say sorry."

"How about a cocktail?" said Manifesto the Great's footman. "Something 'Mae West' like?"

Manifesto the Great stared at his food. "Cocktail?"

"Yes, to wash it down," said Manifesto the Great's footman.

"Wash it down?" said Manifesto the Great.

Manifesto the Great's footman smiled. "Let me see what the cook can knock up; he's excellent with a bit of hemp tea."

Manifesto the Great nodded as a tear slid down his cheek. He felt so empty, hollow like a reed.

Manifesto the Great's footman headed out the door in a state of urgency; his leader was on the point of collapse.

He charged into the kitchen, oblivious to all but the main cook.

"Knock me up something strong, invigorating; damn it, something stimulating," he shouted, silencing the kitchen.

The cook looked at him, confused. "I'm a cook, not a magician."

"The leader," said Manifesto the Great's footman, "has shed a tear."

The kitchen porter, mid filling the pantry, dropped his bag of spuds; the dishwasher, mid dishwashing, switched the taps off; and the peeler, mid peeling, dropped his knife.

"No?" they gasped.

"You sure it's not a cold or something?" said the porter.

"It was definitely a tear," said Manifesto the Great's footman, "and there's more to come, I can tell."

The cook turned to his comrades. "I've heard of men crying," he shook his head. "Damnable thing; once it starts, it's hard to stop."

His comrades nodded.

"I know," sighed Manifesto the Great's footman.

"Who's gonna stand up to those drongo readers if he's crying?" said the dishwasher.

"Exactly," said Manifesto the Great's footman.

The peeler, sensing a crisis of epic proportion, turned to the cook. "You'll need to do something."

"Yes," said the porter. "This is a state of emergency."

"But what?" said the cook. "He's not eating. How can a man think on an empty stomach, let alone stop the tears?"

"That's what I said," said the oaf-like footman, appearing at the doorway.

The staff turned to the large footman filling the doorway.

What is he doing here? thought the cook.

"I wondered about a cocktail, extra strength?" said the oaf-like footman.

Manifesto the Great's footman eyed his comrade. *What would he know?*

The cook ran his finger across his jars of herbs.

"Not them," said the oaf-like footman. "They are as weak as a reader's resolve; you need something that will blast him into action."

The men in the kitchen looked at him.

"Rocket fuel?" said the dishwasher.

The oaf-like footman nodded.

The men crowded around the cook's shelves, eyeballing the containers of herbs and seeds.

"That," said the oaf-like footman, pointing to a jar of soya.

The men gasped.

Soya was new, first designed by the Aliens to cheaply feed the four-legged creatures. However, the institute had modified it to speed up the farm animals' growth and, of course, feed the women rather than precious meat.

"One whiff of that stuff and my woman's bristling about the place like a hen in a field," said the dishwasher. "I have even heard her whistling."

"Whistling?" said the porter. "I managed a bit of bed-diving with my woman."

The peeler whistled through his teeth. "Like waking the dead."

"Why don't you double the quantities?" said the oaf-like footman.

The cook, mid pulling out his blender, stopped. "Nobody doubles a dose and gets away with it."

"Add some hemp, and he'll not know what hit him," said the oaf of a footman.

He smiled at the others.

"He'll be tucking into that meat and back to his old manly self in no time."

Within minutes, Manifesto the Great's footman reappeared by Manifesto the Great's side, panting from an upstairs run.

Not an easy feat when balancing a tray in a tight footman's uniform, slippery heels, and a wig that tended to slump over the eyes.

He slid the tray beside the leader.

"Here, sir; this will warm you up."

Manifesto the Great stared at a large jug decorated like something out of a Bahamas cocktail lounge.

Manifesto the Great's footman handed a glass to his leader. "Down it in an oner," he said. "Works wonders with a meatloaf."

Manifesto the Great obeyed.

The cocktail hit the leader's stomach like a blast of glucose, alcohol, dope, and chilies, sparking up his innards like a firecracker. He felt energized, hungry, and enraged all at once as his stomach revved into action, trumpeting an epic fart, which his footman chose to ignore.

The leader stared at his plate. Juices flooded his mouth with hunger hitting him like a sledgehammer.

Damn it; it looked good.

So good that he wanted to shove it into his mouth in an "oner."

He pushed an obscene forkful into his mouth and gobbled with a "hmmm."

Manifesto the Great's footman watched as he cleared the plate. "How about another?"

Manifesto the Great nodded.

Manifesto the Great's footman, clutching the empty plate, left the room.

He had no idea that thanks to feeding four-legged creatures the new growth food, the city's meat was as toxic as a rat's pee.

So toxic that plates of the stuff would "head-flatten" even the smartest of men, but then no one did. In fact, no one had any idea of "head-flattening" until it was too late.

Manifesto the Great drained his glass and poured another, waiting impatiently for his next plateful. He was so hungry he couldn't think of anything else, let alone bother with the Librarian who had just entered with a dramatic door-scraping of his wheelchair.

Normally, Manifesto the Great would have tutted and swore; he did neither. He just stared at his empty fork, then poured another cocktail.

The Librarian, curious, circled the room, crashing into as much furniture as possible, waiting for a reaction.

Manifesto the Great sighed, drained his glass, then twirled his empty fork in front of him like he was pondering a great philosophical truth.

"How long does it take for a footman to run up and down those stairs?" he muttered.

The Librarian stared at him, then scraped his wheelchair along the side of Manifesto the Great's desk.

Manifesto the Great sucked his fork.

The Librarian crunched over his toes, forcing eye contact with his leader.

Manifesto the Great snapped. "What do you want?"

"They have passed the proposal," said the Librarian.

"Who?" said Manifesto the Great, draining his glass.

"Who do you think?" said the Librarian. "The readers."

"Oh . . . well . . . good luck to them."

Manifesto the Great stopped. "Wait a minute. What proposal?"

"The filtering system," said the Librarian.

"Filtering system?" said Manifesto the Great. He filled his glass. "Is there a blockage somewhere?"

"No," snapped the Librarian, "it is the new name for that policy."

Manifesto the Great looked confused.

"The one you didn't like?" said the Librarian.

Manifesto the Great gulped his drink, wondering where that footman was with his seconds—he hadn't eaten for days.

The Librarian waited for a reaction.

Manifesto the Great's stomach rumbled.

"The policy," snapped the Librarian.

"What policy?" said Manifesto the Great.

"The breeding policy," said the Librarian. "The one I warned against."

Chapter Eleven

COCKTAILS

"The memory of a computer is useless without the password."– The Mae West robot

Manifesto the Great's footman, with a gentle knock, entered the room with a "sir."

The two men stopped as Manifesto the Great's footman silently slid a plate by Manifesto the Great's elbow.

The Librarian stared at the large meatloaf slice oozing cheese, garnished with a prawn fish salad smothered in pink dressing.

It was the sort of food rarely seen apart from celebration days.

Manifesto the Great's footman eyed the empty jug.

"More cocktails, sir?" said Manifesto the Great's footman.

Manifesto the Great nodded.

Manifesto the Great's footman, with a crisp click of his heels, left the room.

The Librarian watched as Manifesto the Great slid his fork into the prawn and dipped it into the sauce.

"Easy on that stuff," he hissed.

Manifesto the Great, ignoring him, pressed more food onto his fork.

"Too much, and you'll be talking bollocks like those idiot readers," said the Librarian.

Manifesto the Great ignored him. He had spent years listening to that claptrap from his mother, and it was the last thing he wanted to hear from that old codger. He filled his mouth, licking his lips as pink sauce dribbled down his chin.

Munching on a chop was but a distant memory for the Librarian. An elderly man with the digestion of a worm and the teeth of a bulimic, he spent his days tucking into mashed bananas and the like, his head as clear as waterfall water.

The Librarian first noticed the effects of meat after a "let's celebrate being a reader" barbecue that the readers had most months.

No sooner were they chomping into burgers and they were talking gibberish, toasting bygone leaders and laughing at terrible jokes about the footmen.

After several burgers and plates of fish, the readers were behaving like buffoons.

"That'll be the head-flattening," tutted an old woman clearing the plates. "My man always acts like that after a stew, like someone's squashed his brain."

"Cop this," yelled a reader, imitating Manifesto the Great's dwarf-like statue by walking on his knees.

The others fell about, laughing.

The old woman shook her head.

"Just wait till the paranoia sets in; my man thinks the Aliens have bugged the Mae West robots, won't even let one in the house," she said, and, with a shake of her head, she wheeled her trolley away.

The Librarian stared at his leader, gulping food like a Labrador.

He pulled the plate away.

"I said, easy on that stuff; indigestion leads to stupid decisions."

Manifesto the Great pulled the plate back.

"I'll decide what to eat," he said.

"Your mother would have chosen a pear over a prawn any day."

"Yeah, and look where it got her," snapped Manifesto the Great.

"She did live to see many things," said the Librarian. "Without . . ." He looked down at his wheelchair. ". . . aids."

"*Pfff*, what would you know?" said the leader.

The Librarian huffed, sparking a coughing fit that would put even a famine victim off their food.

"Know?" coughed the Librarian. "I know that your joints will swell."

Manifesto the Great, a prawn millimeters from his mouth, stopped. "So?"

"And you'll puff up like a balloon." The Librarian grunted between coughs.

Manifesto the Great pulled a face.

"Must you do that here?"

The Librarian began to choke.

Manifesto the Great's footman entered and, in a flash, hammered a heavy pat on the Librarian's back, thrusting a cup under his chin at the same time.

The Librarian filled the mug.

Manifesto the Great looked at his prawn, holding back a gag.

"The puffing up is a mere rumor," said Manifesto the Great's footman.

"Rumor, my arse," the Librarian spluttered.

"And as for the joint swelling—pure conjecture," said Manifesto the Great's footman.

"Bollocks," spat the Librarian, missing the cup.

Manifesto the Great's footman, with disdain, wiped the spit from his sleeve.

"I think it is best to leave the leader at present," said Manifesto the Great's footman and, with a swift push of the wheelchair, marched the Librarian into the corridor.

Manifesto the Great's footman pushed a coughing Librarian down the corridor, swiftly depositing him back in his room.

A room so small that lunging was impossible, so dark a mirror could not be used, and with no view bar the brick wall of an alleyway.

It was a room fit for a man on his last legs, a man that should have pegged it years ago, a man no one noticed, let alone listened to.

As Manifesto the Great's footman silently clicked the door shut behind him, the Librarian glared into the shadows.

"Pickling footman," he muttered.

Beryl, lying in the dark, heard the clutter of the Librarian's wheelchair.

She peered from her pokey room; he was staring at his window.

She had been there several months, and despite the Librarian's dislike of women, she had grown on him.

She was a thinker, a question-asker, and a listener—honey to the Librarian, who for years had been ignored, laughed at, and sometimes even told to "keep it down." Of what, he had no idea, but apparently keeping things "down" was all the rage on Planet Earth.

Beryl knew little about her father, apart from his famed ability to "adapt" and his nickname, "Squirt," which, once she found out why, put her off bed-diving for quite some time.

Squirt died when she was a toddler, before she even got a chance to yell "Daddy" or sit on his knee (which was highly unlikely considering the sort of "chap" he was).

Beryl had vague childhood memories of being tucked away in a dark room, falling asleep to background music and laughter, often woken by the odd man or woman staggering into her room with an "oh?" and leaving just as quickly.

But now she had a teacher, an old man in a wheelchair who happily answered whatever she asked. And the more the Librarian answered, the more she asked.

The Librarian loved it; they spent all their days in the old library. He talked of his time advising the great leaders and of the "dreaded" Wife-ie, the "pain in the arse" Aggie, and the "know it all" LM-2.

Beryl, who had spent years having her questions answered with a "shhh," was not only in school heaven but learning—mainly what not to do. She drank in knowledge like dry sands devoured water. Answers were all she wanted—until, that is, she tasted power; then, she was never the same.

In fact, some would say it was the sparking of the ruthless leader she would become; others say it was the actual falling of Fanny that did it.

Chapter Twelve

ORANGES AND SOCKS

"The tossing of a wig is on par with the tossing of a bra."–The Mae West robot

The Librarian wheeled himself to the slit of a window, stared at the garbage bins rattling in the wind below, and thought of all that he had done for this so-called city.

He had tried to instill some sort of dignity in his leader, warn about the meat, about the women becoming stronger, but Manifesto the Great's mind wandered like an ant across the desert, and all those so-called readers did was jeer him.

Bugger the lot of them, he thought.

He deserved his last hoorah or at least a decent view, and he wasn't going to give that up without a fight.

The Librarian sighed, reversed from the window, and crashed into a table, sending a glass of water flying.

Beryl, jumping from her bed, was by his side in seconds, cleaning up like she had done it for ten years.

"All I need is information they don't have," he said.

"Shall we go to the library?" said Beryl.

"Not that sort." He patted her hand.

"What sort, then?" said Beryl.

He looked at her innocent face. "The sort that people would kill to suppress."

"You mean listening incognito?" said Beryl.

He stopped. "Yes."

"With a disguise?" said Beryl.

The Librarian's face lit up as an idea hit him like a wet fish around the face. Who would question a disabled woman?

He could get away with murder and spy like there was no tomorrow. Not that he wanted to murder anyone, let alone spy. But he could convince his esteemed leader with a ton of facts, save the city, and make those pickling readers eat their words.

"I always wanted to be a woman," he sighed.

Beryl and the Librarian turned to his wig collection, a collection so large he could open a shop with a "buy one get one free" sale and still have a cupboard full a week later.

The Librarian had taken wig-wearing to a new level. It was not only for formal meetings and balcony waving; he even wore his to bed.

He wheeled himself to his wig room and pulled out his best mile-high red wig.

Beryl shook her head.

He tossed it aside.

He pulled a blonde Mae West lookalike wig—a gift from his leader.

He looked at Beryl.

"Too recognizable," she said.

He slid a dark bun-shaped wig on his head.

Beryl pulled a face.

"I need to look like a worker," he said.

"A trolley pusher?" said Beryl.

The Librarian nodded.

She pulled out a scarf and wrapped it around his wig.

He pursed his lips and laughed.

"You look silly," said Beryl.

"Exactly," said the Librarian.

He lifted a bra.

Beryl grabbed several socks.

He grabbed some oranges.

"Socks," said Beryl.

"Oranges," said the Librarian.

She sighed.

Putting on a bra, let alone stuffing it, is not easy for a first-timer, especially in a wheelchair. She tried to help but got in the way. Finally, with an even longer sigh, she stood back and watched as he slapped on red ink for "lippy" like he was drawing a map.

She talked of "toning it down," but the Librarian was too excited to listen.

"Even my mother wouldn't go that red," she said.

The Librarian patted her head. "Spying calls for slapper lips," he said with a sharp turn toward the door.

Beryl stared at his back. "Slapper? That's what they called my mother, and the last thing she did was spy."

"To the canteen," shouted the Librarian with a jocular wave to his protégé and, with his oranges bouncing around like ping-pong balls, he motored out the door.

Beryl, confused, watched as the only person on the planet that she trusted head into the corridor, looking as much like a woman as a gorilla in a suspender.

The footmen in the corridor stifled a smirk. They assumed he was nuts; after all, for months, he had been talking to his invisible "Beryl" friend in the bowels of the old library, even ordering food for two.

"Two oranges do not make a cleavage," said one footman to another, which the Librarian chose to ignore.

"But it sure makes a lunatic happy," said the other, which the Librarian, now out of earshot, didn't hear.

He was heading for the workers' canteen. The future of his beloved city was in the palm of his hands, and he, as sure as pickled eggs, was not going to let it slip away.

Beryl headed to the library; instinct told her oranges weren't the way to go, and she wanted to help.

The library was all she knew. It told her of the past, where she came from.

"Some say your father was a great innovator," said the Librarian.

"Others, a hard-hearted bastard who'd happily sell his aunt down the river."

Beryl thought of her aunts; selling them down the river seemed like a good idea to her. Being in the company of that batch of old crows was as comfortable as trying to sleep at the foot of her father's statue. Even her mother would agree; it was she who called them the "old crows."

Babs, her mother, often cursed them, usually with the vicious stabbing of a smoke butt red with lipstick into a dish or blowing her nails dry.

"Thank pickle you're not like those has-been sardines; you're more like him," she'd say with a drunken gesture toward a hand-size model of Squirt. A trinket that after a particularly drunken night ended headless on the floor, followed by an "oh shit" from Babs.

Babs, it turned out, ran Squirt's Speakeasy. However, it took several years for Beryl to understand what a "speakeasy" was. By that time, they were outlawed, and Manifesto the Great was under the thumb of a completely different room of readers.

Beryl learned of the speakeasy because she heard the gossip and caught a glimpse of the readers, many being the faces of men who walked into her bedroom with an "oh" late at night and left just as quickly.

Beryl entered the old, dark library, moving through the shelves. She ran her fingers along the covers. She had learned of the spaceships, the badlands, the "don't-open gate," and the great gene pool.

The Librarian, ahead of his time, didn't believe in genes. He believed in plotting, scheming, and getting rid of the competition until he looked at Beryl and thought she deserved better.

The Librarian was free with his knowledge, answering all her questions apart from bed-diving—any mention of that word had him choking on his precious caffeine.

"It's complex," said the Librarian, "and power is way more fun."

She looked at the forbidden shelf.

"Innovative shagging."

"Bored? Try a little leather."

"Bed-diving for beginners."

"The musings of a slapper."

And *The Power of Sperm* by James the Strong had Beryl pulling faces and the Librarian wrenching the book from her.

"He claimed it's the answer to everything," said the Librarian, "and look what happened to him."

"Didn't he grow old?" said Beryl.

"Yes, but . . . well," he fumbled with the book, "but not wiser; in fact, he turned into an imbecile."

"Oh, one of them," said Beryl, still confused.

"Yes," snapped the Librarian. He slid the book back.

"Just because someone looks the part—speaks the part—doesn't mean they *are* the part."

Beryl stared at him. "Part?"

"What you need is the ability to reason, design, and, well, diffuse."

"Me, diffuse?" said Beryl, regretting the whole bed-diving conversation.

"The men of Planet Hy Man think power is"—he gestured to his pelvis—"down there."

Beryl sort of understood.

"One day, bed-diving will be as obsolete as a spaceship," he said. "So why worry about it? Bonding is the answer; make a tribe, and before you know it, and you'll have a group who will lay down their lives for you."

Beryl nodded, writing down the words of the Librarian like she understood.

In the end, it was the hoover women laid down for Beryl; life was the last thing on their minds.

Chapter Thirteen

THE LOWERING OF THE FLAG

"Playing requires imagination; imagination while obeying is optional."—The unknown cleaner

Jack and John headed out of the shed, arguing over what to do. They knew Fanny and her entourage would be back.

The arguing was going nowhere, and when Fanny appeared on the horizon, John pushed Jack into the turtle cavity with Jack still arguing.

"I have a plan," he lied.

Only when they got to the city's outskirts did Jack realize John had no plan.

They could hear Fanny making noises, the women preparing to "cavity jump," and Jack could see panic set in John's face. "I told you we shouldn't have taken the turtle," he hissed.

"All right, girls, brace yourself for the jump," yelled Fanny.

The turtle stopped as the women landed with a thud on the ground.

John grabbed Jack's arm and pulled, jumped, and rolled.

Jack swore, stood up, and, as the turtle trotted into the distance, dusted himself off.

"Even I could have thought of that," said Jack.

John said nothing; he was surveying the entrance to the city, wondering which way to go.

"Anyone can make a duck-and-dive plan. In fact, it's not even a plan; it's more a panic," said Jack.

"Shh," said John.

Jack rolled his eyes.

"Listen," said John.

"What?" said Jack.

"They're booing."

It was a fair walk to the center, and as John and Jack made their way through several back alleyways to the marketplace, the booing grew louder. By the time they passed the fruit and vegetable stand, the speech trumpets were in full flow.

John stopped. "Speeches? Now?"

"More bollocks about baby-making," muttered a banana seller.

Jack looked at the speech balcony in the distance and pointed to John. They watched as the flag of Manifesto the Great began to ease down the pole like a pair of loose knickers.

The flag, inspired by war films on the mirror, was not exactly a hit with the locals. They did not see the need for a daily reminder of the leader's face flapping in the wind, but lowering it every day for the past week was just plain pretentious.

It was his mother, after all—an outcast, hardly royalty.

If anything, they should be celebrating, perhaps even get a day off. What they got were a few measly leaflets tossed from the speech balcony about the "rationing of meat."

Like it wasn't already rationed.

A passerby screwed up a leaflet in disgust. "How long can a man live on gristle, albeit battered and fried?"

John and Jack looked at each other. Battered gristle? They thought they had it tough with sandwiches.

The two men watched as the flag flopped to the ground.

"Has our leader died?" said John.

"No," said a passerby, "he's taken to his bed."

"*Pfff*, bed," mumbled another. "Wish I could take to my bed."

"All right for some," muttered the passerby. "My mother died years ago. Do you hear me complaining, waving flags about like a used tissue?"

The chairman looked out of the window onto the market below and shook his head.

"You'd think they be happy."

"Sir?" said the oaf-like footman.

"Well, you know, with a humane leader, a leader who cares, feels, shows mercy."

"Sir, he is sulking while the minions starve," said the oaf-like footman.

The chairman threw a "that's true" look. "When did you get so smart?"

"Listening to you readers," lied the oaf-like footman.

The chairman pulled a crooked smile and turned to the readers engrossed in paperwork; the segregation of women had been signed, sealed, and was merely waiting to be delivered.

"Happy men means a happy city," he said.

A reader looked up. "What was that?"

The chairman rolled his eyes and was on the point of repeating himself when the readers began to moan about how "implementing was thirsty work" and being as "dry as a prune in a desert."

Another, muttering about hunger, reached for a sandwich hidden beneath a sea of paperwork. He nodded to Manifesto the Great's footman with a "beverages now" look.

The oaf-like footman headed out the door, straight into the "room with a view's cleaner," giving the room with a view's specially designed, top-of-the-range Mae West prototype a "what for."

She looked at Manifesto the Great's footman with disdain.

"You know these things are hardly worth the metal they have been recycled from; she talks about 'guns in pockets' and 'being good at being bad.' I am fed up. She's more Mae West than Mae West. Did they have to copy quite so religiously?"

She shoved the top of the range Mae West prototype toward the room with a view.

"Go do some back rubbing and get out of my hair."

And before the oaf of a footman could stop her, the top-of-the-range Mae West prototype was in the room with a view, greasing up like a good old-fashioned English Channel swimmer.

At first, her rubs were appreciated, enjoyed, as the readers pondered and quipped over their paperwork, until she used her elbow and "wired in," as one reader put it.

According to many, a Mae West prototype's elbow was "like a drill," which no amount of "get off" would stop, except the mention of a dump, skip, or any other recycle collecting bin. All Mae West prototypes loved a good rummage in rubbish. It was the metal; they couldn't get enough of the stuff.

The top-of-the-range Mae West prototype sashayed into the room, scanning the shoulders for tension. She had her pick; one look at her, and a man tensed up like his balls were being electrocuted.

None noticed her scanning the paperwork, her photographic eyes blinking snapshots like a paparazzi photographer; they thought it was part of her flirting program.

"That's it," sighed a voice from the back. "I've had it with this paperwork. It's good enough."

"Good enough?" said the chairman. "Good enough is never good enough for the running of things. We need to be as tight as the knot of a pulling rope."

"The only thing tight is my neck bent over this bollocks," said the voice from the back, rubbing his neck.

The Mae West prototype's hands headed for his shoulders. "Tight is my middle name, honey," she said.

"Get off me," snapped the reader.

She moved from shoulder to shoulder, brushed off with a "him," a "no, him," and a "bugger off, will you?"

She stopped at the chairman.

Her hand splayed around the back of his neck.

Silence.

"Are you pleased to see me, or is that a pen?" said the prototype.

The frazzled chairman exploded. "It's a gun, you moronic robot. Now, bugger off."

The Mae West prototype, her files full to the brim with images of the paperwork, sauntered out the door like a prostitute looking for her next trick.

Chapter Fourteen

ANOTHER SHED

"A robot that knows the ropes is likely to be a Mae West prototype."–The Mae West robot

Jack and John tenderly placed their backpacks on the ground and stared at the shed at the back of the institute garden.

On the last of its hinges, the door crashed to the ground, unsettling a few mechanical rats.

They had toyed with the idea of impressing the institute, dreamed of a pension, penthouse, perhaps even a statue, but the institute had laughed at their Petri dishes.

The institute being the receptionist at the front desk, the male worker who had worked his way up from a "foreigner" footman and had eyes on becoming a "white coat" in a lab.

He was so new he had no idea who Jack and John were, let alone that they were called "fruit loops." He sent them away with an "as if?" jibe.

Apart from the cleaner and the Mae West robot, it seemed no one missed them.

To be fair, it had only been a week.

A week where the Mae West robot, completely useless without their help, had piled all the washing in the shed where Jack and John were standing.

They stared at the heap of stained white coats and dishcloths covering months of hidden ropes.

"Well, at least we know what happened to all the rope," muttered John.

He pushed at the pile with his foot; a mechanical rat scurried away.

"With a bit of spit and polish, we could get this up and running," said Jack.

Another rat followed.

"Maybe one of those fridges; every lab has a fridge, and it'd be handy with all these Petri dishes," said Jack.

John looked at Jack. "When did you get so scientific?"

"I've always been scientifically scientific," he said.

A baby rat shot across John's foot.

He stood on its tail.

"We'll need more shelves," he said.

"You always want more shelves," said Jack.

"Well, you can never have enough shelves in a shed," said John, lifting the rat by its tail.

The rat disengaged from its tail, plopped to the ground like a cat, and, with a dignified march, disappeared under the door.

The two men stared at the tail still in John's hand.

"Especially with these critters running around, and we'll need a shelf to account for the dummy run," said John.

"You mean to control Petri dishes," said Jack.

John pretended not to hear.

Under the guise of making compost, Jack and John set things up. It didn't take them long to acquire a rat diverter, a fridge, and a few logs for a fire.

John went to town on the shelves; he recycled everything he could lay his hands on.

They were experienced in setting up labs and soon discovered a talent for recycling. Mae West followed.

She was an expert at skip rummaging; hitching her skirt up, she'd climb into anything remotely metal.

In fact, she would climb into anything for Jack.

The Mae West robot was obsessed with Jack, hell-bent on getting in wherever Jack was, including the shed.

Every day, clutching a tea tray, she entered the garden, focused on her target like a bird of prey, and she would not leave until the men opened the door.

Jack and John tried turning her away, but all she did was turn back. She was like a bomb programmed for its target, and once in the shed, she refused to leave.

One look at Jack peering over a Petri dish, dropper poised, and she was mesmerized. Tea-pouring forgotten, she could not hold herself back.

"Is that a dropper in your hand, or are you pleased to see me?" she'd say, peering over Jack's shoulder.

And when Jack didn't answer, she took to giving him a shoulder rub.

The institute, busy working on a new, improved synthetic animal food, had no idea that there was a garden shed, let alone what Jack and John were up to.

Bette, however, was suspicious.

She'd seen Jack and John loitering outside the shed, redirecting the Mae West robot away from it, erecting washing poles in the garden, tying the Mae West robot to one, and running away like schoolboys.

And that robot, with no mental capabilities whatsoever, never gave up. She stuck like glue to those men, even when they disappeared to god knows where and arrived back full of junk.

That robot even helped them carry said junk into the shed.

And as for the shed, it had turned from some rat-infested, run-down eyesore to a pristine building with a door that clicked shut and what looked like a small fire in the back.

In three days?

What in the name of sperm was going on?

After a week, Bette had had enough.

She grabbed her master key, sneaked down the garden, barged in like a storm trooper, and gasped.

"Ooh, arrrrgh," sighed Jack.

The Mae West robot, kneading Jack's shoulders like a bread maker, continued.

"Just there," said Jack.

"What the ectoplasm is going on?" yelled Bette.

Jack looked up.

The Mae West robot stopped as John appeared from their new rear entrance, wiping his hands on his pilfered cook's apron.

Bette glared at John's apron. "And who said you could use that?"

"White coats are hard to come by," mumbled John.

"White coats? What do you need white coats for?"

The Mae West robot returned to her kneading, this time with her elbow.

John launched into his rehearsed "we're making compost" story, which was greeted with a "don't make me laugh" from the cleaner.

"I know you two boys, and let me tell you, the last thing you'd be doing is making pickling compost."

"Okay," snapped John, "you've caught us making home brew." And before he could launch into his second "if the first story doesn't work" story, the cleaner began to cackle.

"Home brew?" she jeered. "If that's home brew, I am a headless statue."

"You haven't seen our home brew, though, have you?" said Jack, wincing as the Mae West robot's elbow hit a nerve.

"What sort of home brew is your home brew, then?" said Bette.

"You'll have to wait and see," said John.

"Now you're making me split my sides; look, the tears are running down my cheeks," said Bette.

She looked about the shed; she had dusted a few labs, seen a few embryos . . .

"There is only one thing a Petri dish is used for, especially with a Bunsen burner."

"Home brew?" said John.

"Don't make me split my sides again," said Bette. "The last thing that Petri dish is growing is the likes of home brew."

She stopped. She had found something—something that had nothing to do with home brew. Maybe she could use this something?

Bette had heard the speeches of segregation, and she, like many women, was at the point of rebellion.

Her mother was a great breeder, her sister as prolific as a rabbit, and she, a young upwardly mobile cleaner, had the same robust pelvis. She'd be expected to bed-dive like there was no tomorrow. Not a prospect she jumped for joy at. In fact, she'd rather have a sandwich full of gristle than a man between her legs.

She had to play it cool, not intimidate, but confuse the truth out of them.

With her famous "I'm waiting for an answer" glare, she crossed her arms.

"Tea?" said John, gesturing to the pot.

"Seat?" said Jack.

"Back rub?" said the Mae West robot.

Bette, with her best "our Bette" smile, took a seat, watched John pour while pushing Mae West away at the same time.

She downed her tea, pondering.

She had heard of an underground "women for women by women" sort of thing, but she had also heard that they had become selective, thanks to a few "kiss and tell" cleaners.

One look at a cleaner's uniform and they were shown the door, with a "here's your hat, what's your hurry" shove.

Well, she thought, *two can play at that game.*

She eyed the Petri dishes. If these men were doing what she thought they were doing, then she knew of a way to not only get into this so-called selective underground but have 'em begging, on their knees.

She drained her tea, eyed John, and said, "Have you heard of a woman called Fanny?"

John choked on his tea as Jack completely missed his target with his dropper.

"Fanny?" said the Mae West robot. "Well, when she's good, she's good, but when she's bad, she's even better."

Chapter Fifteen

THE CANTEEN

"The best way to hold a robot is with lubrication."–The Mae West robot

The Librarian entered the canteen, his squeaky wheelchair silencing the chatter like the entrance of a naked woman.

No one had seen a wheelchair in the workers' quarters apart from the Librarian. Disabled people were kept out of sight, behind desks, making toys for children—a business that had seriously dried up.

The cleaners eyed him.

A footman sniggered.

"Didn't know the Librarian had a sister," said a cleaner.

"He doesn't," said the sniggering footman.

The Librarian adjusted his wig, ran his tongue along his red lips, and surveyed the canteen—a place as new to him as the queue about the counter, as foreign as a footman not standing to attention.

He stared at one lounging by the window.

The oaf-like footman stared back with no sign of averting his eyes.

The Librarian turned away and realized he had never seen a footman lounge before, let alone a cleaner free of a mop, a trolley, or that other thing—a broom?

He watched as a cleaner by the watercooler, flipped the tap closed, sipped her drink, then moved to her table full of cleaners.

Her eyes never left his.

The Librarian averted his eyes yet again, feeling as vulnerable as a mouse under the eyes of a cat.

The canteen wasn't his first thought—Fanny's underground was—but after several abortive efforts to cross the main street busy with speeding transporters, he gave up.

He had no idea there were so many transporters, nor that his wig had as much ability to withstand the wind of a speeding transporter as a canary in a hurricane.

In fact, thanks to the regular gusts of winds, he looked like a drag queen electrocuted several times, and his ability to stop a passerby was on par with a road accident; even the racing transporters were tooting at him.

"Who the hell is that?" said a passerby.

"Him with the crazy wigs," said another. "I heard he's gone mad."

The Librarian, catching a glimpse of himself in the window, stopped, even he thought he looked crazy. His chances of incognito road-crossing were slimmer than a four-legged creature making it to puberty.

He headed back into the worker's entrance, and, with a futile wig pat, made for the canteen.

If anyone was going to believe his disguise, it would be the workers.

The canteen was jam-packed with footmen and cleaners: a big mistake by the readers.

The readers—assuming that a low job meant a low IQ, that women and estrogen equaled brain fog, and that any man wearing an outfit as stupid as a footman's just had to be equally stupid—never thought of the inevitable: the underdogs, despite their different costumes, would join forces.

Not even the Librarian saw that coming, until, that is, he tried to eat in the canteen.

A cleaner's outfit was as unattractive as a footman's, ridiculous, yet standing in a queue waiting for the same rubbish food united them.

Especially when they heard of the barbecues held for the "elite," as the readers liked to call themselves.

"We need food for our brains," claimed the readers, and as Manifesto the Great's footman watched the so-called brain food send the reader "gaga," they began to think outside the box, something many workers had a gift for.

It was the boredom of their duties that did it. Thanks to the increase of robots, a footman's duty had been reduced to standing around pretending not to listen, while a cleaner's was more pushing about equipment pretending not to hear.

The Librarian stared at the queue of footmen, unsure of what to do. He watched as a cleaner joined and decided to follow.

He inched closer; the cleaner picked up a tray and slapped it on the bench like she had done a million times before.

The Librarian followed; not easy when your nose is the level of the bench.

As the line passed by the hot steaming mash, he sniffed.

Nothing, thought the Librarian. Not even a hint of what was steaming from the hot plate, not even a whiff to wet his lips.

He squeaked closer, wondering what the hell they ate.

"Same old rubbish, then?" a footman teased the cook.

"Mind your manners," snapped the red-faced woman.

The Librarian, with a clear view of her stomach, watched as a spoonful of mush plopped onto a plate.

Manifesto the Great's footman, a slim man, slid the plate onto his tray and moved to a table.

The Librarian pushed his tray toward the stomach; the cook bent to his eye level.

"Never seen you before."

"I'm here to assist the Librarian," he squeaked in his best female voice.

A few snickered from behind.

"Well, that explains the wig," muttered the cook.

More snickering.

"Is that one of his?" said a cleaner from the table.

"Well, yes," squeaked the Librarian, pulling a girlie face.

"Stupid man," huffed the cook, slapping mush onto a plate. She slid the plate to the Librarian.

"Mae West robot not good enough for him?" laughed a footman from behind.

"Well, yes. I mean, err, no."

"What does that idiot need an assistant for?" said the cook.

"To change his pants," laughed a voice from behind.

The Librarian, with a sharp turn that had the voice jumping out of the way, snapped, "I change my own—"

He stopped as the face of a large oaf-like footman stared at him.

"I'm more admin," he said, "files, that sort of thing."

Manifesto the Great's footman stared at the wheelchair. "You a magician?"

"Leave the poor thing alone," said the cook.

The Librarians turned; several workers jumped out of the way.

The cook caught his eye.

"Don't let that fool of a man take advantage; just because he's in a wheelchair don't mean—"

She stopped, blushed.

"Here, have some extra. On the house." She inched closer, her red lips almost touching the Librarian's face. "And don't get the pudding," she whispered. "It's been about four days."

The cook gestured to the kitchen behind her. "Herself over there is not herself."

"Herself?" said the Librarian.

"The pudding maker," snapped the cook.

There's a maker of puddings? thought the Librarian.

"She's never herself," muttered Manifesto the Great's footman from behind.

"Never," said another.

The cook threw a caustic glare at Manifesto the Great's footman.

"Her man's a 'pouncer,' what do you expect?" She turned to the Librarian. "You know the sort, love?" She eyed the wheelchair. "Perhaps not."

The Librarian nodded like he knew what she was talking about, like he knew what a pouncer was.

He hadn't a clue.

A cleaner, catching the Librarian's "what the pickle" face, yelled, "A pouncer is the sort of knob that pounces on a woman like a wild animal. He bed-dives like a cowboy taming a horse, no warm-up, no 'do you fancy it?'"

"In and out like a toilet brush," grumbled the cook.

The Librarian, with weird images of toilet brushes and cowboys and an equally weird plate of whatever balanced on his knee, looked about for a table.

"Here, Miss," said a cleaner, gesturing to a space between her and several other cleaners.

"Join us. Us women need to stick together." She laughed.

The others giggled.

"If that's a woman, then I'm pregnant," said another cleaner.

"That could be arranged," said the slim footman.

"In your dreams," blushed the cleaner, who had been barren for several years.

Chapter Sixteen

CAUGHT

"Never judge a robot by its quotes."–The Mae West robot

It didn't take long for the Librarian to realize they all knew who he was as soon as he entered the canteen; apparently, the oranges gave it away; and the lipstick.

The funny thing was the Librarian didn't care.

He liked the idea that his prodigy was right, that he had taught her well. Besides, a dress liberated him, especially when everyone knew that underneath was a man.

He began to camp it up big-time, and the more women laughed, the more he enjoyed himself.

He had never enjoyed himself before.

His life had been one of manipulation and arse-licking. He had no idea how delicious fun was, just as he had no idea that women could be so entertaining. He thought they were all like LM-2 and Aggie, bossy know-it-alls with not only an answer for everything but a caustic look that could stifle an argument quicker than a gas leak could clear a room.

These women were different; sure, they had a few muscles and rugged voices, but they giggled and laughed at everything he said.

"How was I to know that putting on lipstick was an acquired talent?" he quipped more than once.

They fell about laughing.

Then, when an orange plopped onto the ground, the women nearly wet themselves.

"Two oranges do not make a cleavage," joked the Librarian, which even had the "not herself" cook wiping tears of laughter from her eyes.

The footmen watched, unsure of all this hilarity, some muttering about pinching jokes.

"What's a man in a dress got that we haven't?" mumbled one.

"Well, a dress for a start," cackled the cook.

The Librarian looked at the cook. Her flash of kindness had almost touched him.

He wondered what would happen to her when all this segregation started. Would she be lumbered with a pouncer?

"We need a revolution," he said. "A revolt, an uprising. Those readers will ruin this city."

Silence.

The workers looked at the Librarian, his wig as squint as a sinking flagpole, as lopsided as a sinking ship; one wrong move and it would perch on his shoulder like a pirate's parrot.

"What would he know?" said the oaf-like footman. "Him who set the animals free."

"We all make mistakes," said the Librarian.

"Mistakes? You caused a rampage. It took weeks to clear up that dung."

"It was good for the gardens," muttered the Librarian.

Silence.

He bent to pick up his orange; it rolled from his reach.

"I don't see any plants complaining," he grunted.

The cook jumped to help and slid the orange onto the Librarian's lap.

"Just shows you know bugger all," said the oaf-like footman.

"I know that they are talking of segregation," said the Librarian.

The "not herself" cook in the kitchen dropped a tray. "I'll never get a good night's sleep again," she grumbled.

"Segregation?" said the oaf-like footman. "That old chestnut."

"It ain't old, and it's no chestnut," said Manifesto the Great's footman, appearing at the doorway.

The canteen silenced as he strolled through like he was in a Western.

His comrades rolled their eyes. Being the personal footman of the leader had, to an extent, gone to his head; well, that and looking pretty good in a tight pair of trousers.

A cleaner sighed; another nudged her.

Manifesto the Great's footman looked at the Librarian—as convincing as a woman as the soya mash was enjoyable.

"He's right. We can't let them rule."

The Librarian, spluttering his tea, began to cough.

"I've been saying that for years," lied the oaf-like footman.

"You?" snorted the cook.

The Librarian continued to cough; a few began to pull a face as the coughing turned to a gag.

Manifesto the Great's footman, with a curt thrust of a mug under the Librarian's chin, administered a brisk thump.

Another cleaner sighed.

"Show-off," mumbled the oaf-like footman.

Manifesto the Great's footman adjusted the Librarian's wig.

The Librarian, with an "I can do it" shove, turned to his audience.

"I could create a diversion." He coughed again. "While you—" He spluttered. "You know . . ."

"What?" snapped a voice from the back.

The Librarian spat into his cup. "While you cause an uprising."

"Well, as long as you get rid of that getup," said the voice from the back as the oaf-like footman slid out the door.

Jack and John had planned a big revealing, a lavish surprise with their first baby.

"Just think," said John, mid shelf-erecting, "we'll be in white coats again, sipping delicious caffeine, giving orders rather than taking them, and men and women will be happy again, shagging for the fun of it."

"Don't make me laugh," said Bette. "Sex for fun?"

She stopped as the Mae West robot crashed into her from behind with a tray.

"Men are like carpets," said the Mae West robot. "Lay 'em right, and you can walk all over them for years."

"It's linoleum," said Bette.

"Just pour the tea," said Jack.

The Mae West robot thumped the tray onto a bench and moved to Jack's shoulders. She was desperate to impress, and, thanks to the Mae West prototype, she had just the thing.

John, hammer aimed at a nail, stopped.

The Mae West robot slid her hands onto Jack's shoulders. "It's not what I do, but the way I do it. It's not what I say, but the way I say it."

"Get off me," he spluttered.

She stopped. "Your mind is your weapon; keep it open."

"That's not Mae West," said Bette.

The Mae West robot, leaning on Jack for aim, switched her head to a projector.

Across the shelves projected the photography taken by the room with a view's Mae West prototype . . . and it didn't take long for the two men and the cleaner to decipher the disjointed images spread across the Petri dishes.

Chapter Seventeen

THE CHAIRMAN

"From an early age, Manifesto the Great loved to write things, and, despite technology, did it with a quill. The feather tip made him happy; others said it made him look mad."–Aggie's Greenhouse Guide

It took several days for Manifesto the Great to leave his room, but when he did, he headed straight to the room with a view.

"Let's have a barbecue," he shouted.

He had this vision of a fantastic hunt, followed by an even more fantastic barbecue. Not that he had ever been on a hunt, but he had this desire for a great day, and under the influence of a full stomach, he had no idea how ridiculous it sounded.

There was bugger-all to hunt.

The readers, all ten of them, were sitting at a table covered in piles of files. They looked up, pens poised, and stopped.

It occurred to them that their leader was mad.

"Don't you remember the 'do not open' gate?" said the elderly reader with a look of disdain.

"Oh, that? We can knock it down. Better yet, get a rope and pull it as my grandpappy did."

"Grandpappy?" said a voice from the back.

"Don't you mean 'dad'?" said the elderly reader.

"Yes, and that too." The leader smiled.

He looked at the plate of bananas and was about to shout, "Come with me; I'll give you something to fill your boots!" when the chairman entered, silencing all with a swift flick of his hand.

"Perhaps some signing before beverages?" the chairman said to the leader.

He nodded to the readers, sending them into a flurry of paper-rustling.

Manifesto the Great watched the readers jump to the orders of the chairman, and a thought struck him. Wasn't *he* the leader?

He tapped his foot with impatience.

"Chair?" said the elderly reader.

"Banana?" said the chairman's sidekick.

"How about I rustle you up a sandwich?" said the oaf of a footman.

The chairman threw him a look; the oaf of a footman threw one back, while the elderly reader, looking from one to the other, wondered what the pickle was going on.

Manifesto the Great didn't stay long. He had the attention span of a toddler, an alcoholic thirst for cocktails, and the hunger of a bulimic. His mental state was on edge, and as the oaf of a footman led him away in search of the perfect sauce, the readers looked at each other.

"He's a fruit loop," said the young reader, reaching for a sandwich.

"Don't touch!" shouted the chairman. "Hormones."

"Hormones? What in the name of sperm is a hormone doing in a sandwich?" glared the elderly reader.

"You may well ask," said the chairman.

"I am," he said.

The chairman tossed a bunch of bananas down the table. "Best to stick to things that need peeling. Leave the gaga food for our esteemed leader."

"Gaga food?" said the young reader. "What the ectoplasm are you talking about?"

The chairman talked of the good old days when four-legged creatures ate "stuff from the ground" until, that is, some bozo decided to change the feed.

"Was that not us?" said a voice from the back, which no one bar the elderly reader heard.

Some of the readers grew bored; one even yawned.

Meat withdrawals can do that to a fella; so could the chairman's lectures. He had the monotones of a computer-generated voice and two volumes: "can you speak up" and "waking the dead."

The readers stared at the bananas now scattered about the table.

The young reader picked up one and looked at it. "How long are we to eat bananas for?"

"How long is a piece of pulling rope?" said the chairman's sidekick.

No one laughed.

The chairman's sidekick reached for a banana, peeled it, then slid it between his lips, feigning an "mm."

The young reader followed. "Bananas—they are barbecue-able, aren't they?"

"Absolutely," said the oaf-like footman, filling the doorway.

The young reader looked at his banana. He took a tentative mouthful and pulled a face, then, wrapping the skin around the rest of the banana, put it back on the plate.

"Don't put it back," snapped the elderly reader.

"It's yuck-like," mumbled the young reader through a full mouth.

The readers stared at the gooey stump like it was a severed head.

"Head-flattening," said the chairman in his waking-the-dead voice, "is no myth."

A few jolted. "Head-flattening?"

The chairman nodded. "It's official; our leader has been head-flattened."

"I've been eating flesh for years, and there's nothing wrong with my head," said a voice from the back. "And I shall continue to do so."

He bit into his sandwich, belched, then trumpeted the sort of fart that had many haw-hawing.

"A sauce, a sauce, my kingdom for a sauce," yelled Manifesto the Great from the corridor.

The voice from the back looked at the string of flesh suspended from the corner of his sandwich; he slid it between the crusts.

With an "I'll get that, sir," the oaf of a footman jumped to attention.

The door shut behind him as Manifesto the Great began a chorus of "oh to my giblets."

Silence.

The readers shifted uncomfortably. It was not a pretty sound.

The voice from the back returned his sandwich to its plate.

"Let's put the swords back where they came from, shall we, sir?" said the oaf of a footman.

The chairman eyed his comrades. "Perhaps," he smiled, "kidnapping the leader is no longer called for."

The chairman's cryptic comments of kidnapping went over the readers' heads, apart from the elderly reader. And while the others argued over the various ways to barbecue a banana, he wondered about many things.

Mostly, why the oaf-like footman was suddenly so nice.

It wasn't long before Manifesto the Great took to pacing like his father and talking of women as harlots. In fact, he began to emulate James the Strong, calling him a hero while ignoring any advice.

He embraced what he used to condemn like a lunatic for no reason.

"We need sauces," said the leader, "and sausages," giving even the most hardened readers indigestion.

The readers saw their chance and grasped it; rounding up the women was just the beginning.

The footmen watched in dismay (apart from the oaf-like footman, an expert at sitting on the fence).

"What next?" said Manifesto the Great's footman. "The segregation of workers?"

The footmen, inflamed, whispered in corners of riots and protests, meetups and overthrowing.

A revolution was in the making, and notes (code name: shopping lists) were passed about like Christmas cards via the cleaner's trolley and market stalls.

The uprising was building; timing was crucial.

"We have to make a move," scrawled a footman above a cleaning list, many still unsure just what that move was.

Chapter Eighteen

DIVERSIONS

"An uprising by any other name still requires paperwork."–Fanny

The Librarian had taken to diverting like the proverbial duck to water. Inspired by the suffragettes of past years, he chained himself to a shelf, or rather ordered Beryl to do so.

"I'm moving in here." He coughed.

Beryl, with an expert "clapping" on his back, handed him a tissue.

"I am going to divert like there is no tomorrow," he shouted. "Give those bozos a run for their soya."

"Divert?" said Beryl, fumbling with an out-of-date lock.

"Yes, and your job is to send out a message without being seen."

"How do I do that?"

The Librarian talked of "thinking out of the box." "That's what the suffragettes did, and look where it got them."

Beryl blinked, confused.

He coughed again, sparking a series of gagging.

She held a glass to his lips.

"You're too young to remember." He spat. "The first sightings of the mirror were of Earth women with fire in their eyes."

Beryl stopped; women with fire in their eyes were as foreign to her as a sober mother.

A few days later . . .

Fanny looked out of the window of the "underground headquarters," or "sector one," as she liked to call it. Others called it a basement with a few out-of-date filing cabinets hijacked from a skip.

Filing cabinets were unlike anything on Earth and, for many years, had been a curse on Planet Hy Man.

The filing cabinet was the first in a long line of oral commanding equipment leading to such things as robots in a variety of sizes and just as many smartarse comments, speaking pads that knew the answer to everything but never waited to be asked, and clocks that were, well, clocks with a shouting device that didn't comprehend "shut up."

Fanny's filing cabinets were voice-operated, responding to "open" in its various forms, sparking the "jumping" of drawers, the propelling of files, a mess on the floor, and a fair amount of "pickle" swearing.

LM-2 knocked on the door.

"It's open," shouted Fanny.

The filing cabinets sprang into action.

"Shit," muttered Fanny.

LM-2, like she had done many times before, pushed open the door to find a sea of files on the floor.

"Must you yell that dreaded word?" she hissed.

"What else does a woman say when the door is, well—"

A drawer edge opened, poised for the command.

LM-2 glared a "don't say it" look.

The shelf creaked shut.

LM-2 bent to pick up the mess on the floor while Fanny, a woman from "the right side of the tracks," watched.

She had no idea of such things as "picking up."

She had a husband she hardly saw, an annoying Mae West prototype robot, and absolutely no idea what a broom was for.

Fanny, oblivious to LM-2's "don't worry, I'll pick it up" jibes, stared across at the old library, pondering Aggie's funeral.

"Those Aliens really know about death, don't they?" she said.

"They are not called Aliens anymore," grunted LM-2, mid picking up.

"I've been thinking about Aggie's burial," said Fanny.

"Burning," snapped LM-2, shoving files into a drawer.

"And the bonfire," said Fanny.

"Roasting," said LM-2, slamming a drawer.

"Now, that's how I want to go," sighed Fanny. "Piled high on yesterday's recycling with not a bit of plastic in sight."

"So you keep saying," sighed LM-2.

Fanny turned to LM-2. "That woman died with pride."

"She was good at picking things up, too, so I heard," said LM-2.

A shadow flashed across the windows in the old library.

"Looks like there's movement," said Fanny.

LM-2, with a "hmmm," slid a file under her arm, then cursed as the papers fell out.

Fanny eyed LM-2. "Thought you said it'd been shut down?"

"Yes, well, that's before the Librarian fell out with the leader."

Fanny stopped. "They fell out?"

"Yes, and he's holding a protest. Apparently, he was caught spying in a cleaner's wig and laughed at. He's locked his wheelchair to an old bookcase and is refusing to let anyone in. He says, if the suffragettes can do it, so can he."

Fanny sighed; she loved the suffragettes.

LM-2 bent down to pick up more files. "Apparently, he is a fan," she grunted.

"Hardly," said Fanny.

LM-2 looked up from the mess on the floor. "He is—"

"If he's a fan, I'm a burnt bra," snapped Fanny. "No man admires a suffragette, least of all that bozo."

"Yes, but he's getting about like a woman now," said LM-2.

"With an imaginary friend," said Fanny.

She pulled out her binoculars and focused on the library.

"What on earth is he protesting about?"

"If you gave me a hand, I'd tell you," said LM-2.

"The only thing he'd protest about is the heat of his caffeine," said Fanny.

LM-2 shoved another file into a drawer. "As I said, if you'd help me . . ."

"He just wants to open up old wounds," said Fanny.

A drawer flew open.

LM-2 shut it with her hip. "It's the breeding program," she said.

"Breeding program?" said Fanny.

"It has been reassessed as imperative," said LM-2.

"Reassessed? Imperative? That means—" Fanny stopped.

A drawer inched open.

LM-2 slammed it shut.

"It's because the kindergartens are empty, isn't it?" said Fanny.

"Well, yes."

"They want to weed out the baby-makers, don't they?"

"I have heard of a spreadsheet," said LM-2, "with birthdays."

Fanny shot her a look.

"They are calling women of a certain age 'past their sell-by date,'" said LM-2.

"Well, this is definitely a cause for an uprising," huffed Fanny.

"That's what the Librarian said," sighed LM-2.

Fanny stared into her binoculars. "Besides, the sell-by date will probably include me. And the last thing I want to do is garden or, god forbid, tidy things up."

"I can see that," grunted LM-2, mid bend.

Fanny turned to LM-2 and caught a glimpse of her slim behind, mid picking up.

"Even you're past your sell-by date, not that you were ever in it. That skinny behind of yours has as much chance of breeding as a Mae West robot. In fact, there is a file about who's breed-able somewhere," said Fanny.

"Yes, by your feet," said LM-2.

"Oh," said Fanny. She stared down at the file with "Breeding" scribbled across the front.

She bent to pick it up.

"It says here that our esteemed leader is dead set against the idea," said Fanny. "In fact, he is quoted as calling it outrageous."

"Yes, but our esteemed leader is pigging out on meat, barbecuing like there's no tomorrow. He has as much interest in the breeding project as the city has in the Librarian's wigs."

Fanny began to read the file. She looked up at LM-2. "It's pure and utter segregation."

"That's what the Librarian said," said LM-2.

"Women like me will be sent to the laundry," said Fanny.

"He said that, too."

Fanny stopped. "The Librarian?"

"'Women over the hill will be farmed out like chickens,' he said."

Fanny nodded. "Like you and me."

"I am hardly as over the hill as you," said LM-2.

"You're no spring chicken," said Fanny.

"If I'm no spring chicken, then you're a mere carcass," snapped LM-2.

Fanny returned to her binoculars. "We must stop them," she said.

"Too late," said LM-2. "They've passed the bill."

Chapter Nineteen

SNEAKING AROUND

"A memo by any name still requires that sticky bit."–Beryl

With the ingenuity of an ad agency, Beryl had a way with memos and hiding in corners, a heady talent for an ambitious ten-year-old with time on her hands and a dying Librarian chained to a bookshelf.

It didn't take her long to find the locker rooms. A piece of piss, really, as the locker rooms were along the old library's corridor.

Beryl heard it all, the whispers and the footsteps, while holding a straw to the Librarian silently sipping. Soon, she was wondering about the "Wife-ie Chronicles" and her famed memos in the spaceship.

"Wife-ie's memo has set a lot of things in motion," Beryl said to her mentor.

The Librarian nodded with a slurp. "You learn quick," he said.

A couple of footmen jostled outside the corridor; one tripped the other up.

"Get away with yer," laughed the other.

Beryl wiped the Librarian's lips.

It was night; the cleaners could be heard down the corridor, packing away their trolleys, making quips about tight trousers and large hands.

The Librarian closed his eyes; she covered him with a blanket and slid out into the dark corridor.

With the stealth of a leopard and a pocket full of memos, Beryl entered the footmen's locker room and, with her pen torch, found what she was looking for.

She slid a memo into each of the footmen's lockers and listened.

The cleaners were clearing up, rattling their trolleys back into cupboards.

She waited.

A few giggled, a door slammed.

Silence.

She skirted up the corridor; the cleaners' trolley was a mere skip away.

Verruca watched her mother like she did every morning. Her mother treated her like a comrade even though she was only ten. Verruca, like Beryl, was the last generation to come from a man.

Her father was always in the distance, busy making a "buck or two" as he put it, but every now and then, she'd see him—or rather hear him, usually arguing with her mother. The "filtering scheme" being one of the latest arguments.

This morning, it was particularly bad. So bad that he didn't even say goodbye to her; he skulled his caffeine and slammed the door, pushing past the Mae West prototype like she was the enemy.

And her dad loved that prototype; he laughed at everything she said. Silly things about "guns in pocket" and "coming up to see" whatever.

Her dad always laughed, usually as out loud as a trumpet, often slapping his thighs, which always led her mother to throw "a wobbly" as he put it.

As the prototype's tray crashed to the ground, Verruca's mother fumed.

"That is it," she snapped.

The prototype circled Verruca protectively.

Verruca watched her mother head into her room and pulled out her playthings.

"What are you looking for, Mum?" she said.

Her mother stopped to touch her daughter's face. "Call me Fanny," she said.

"I like Mum," said Verruca.

"It's Fanny," said Fanny, grabbing a few spray cans of paint and shoving them into her daughter's "a robot is not just for birthdays" backpack.

Fanny headed down the corridor talking of "Maisie" and other women.

"Men," said the prototype, "are like buses. There is always another passing by."

"I heard that," shouted Fanny from another room, appearing a few minutes later dressed as a cat burglar (although no-one on Planet Hy Man had heard of one).

She stopped and looked at the sweet face of her daughter. She wanted to protect her from all this procreation bollocks and give her a better world to live in.

"If men are only interested in procreation, then they could whistle for it," said Fanny.

"Procreation?" said Verruca.

"No romance, no bedding." She smiled at her daughter.

She kissed her daughter's forehead, mentioned something about not waiting up, and headed out the door with a slam.

Verruca knew where she was going; it wasn't the first time she'd followed.

Verruca slid outside and followed her mother—and, just like her mother, was completely unaware that someone else, incognito, would see all.

Beryl was in the library when Verruca headed out to follow her mother.

The Librarian was proud of her, making her feel like a true golden statue. Diverting had taken it out of him. He was fading, yet when he looked at his prodigy, he felt as alive as that day in the café, entertaining with his set of oranges.

Beryl held a straw to his lips; he sipped the sparkling water, his favorite.

Beryl looked out the window and caught sight of Verruca heading down the street with purpose. She watched like a child watches a fly on a window, not thinking much of it until a crowd formed, engulfing the girl and pointing at the library . . . or, rather, above it.

Manifesto the Great's footman opened his locker; a memo fluttered to the ground. He stopped to pick it up; the oaf of a footman got there first.

"Well, looky here," he said. "The postman's been."

He thrust the memo under Manifesto the Great footman's nose.

Bugger, thought Manifesto the Great's footman, feigning a "well really" smile.

Chapter Twenty

THE MARKETPLACE

"They didn't bank on the Mae West robot. No one did."–Footman unknown

Bette's Mae West robot stopped at a rope stall as Bette moved on to the banana stall nearby.

"What do you think of this for a small loaf?" she said with a wave of a banana.

She stopped and turned to find her Mae West robot staring at a long piece of paper.

"Gimme that," she said with a tug, causing the Mae West robot to topple on her heels.

Bette looked at the paper, a shopping list that made as much sense as her Mae West robot's high heels, heels so high that hanging out washing gave her vertigo.

Bette eyed the stall owner, a young man with a blank face and little behind it. He ran the store for his elders and had no idea or interest in cleaning fluids. In fact, he had no idea of anything other than that he was hungry, and there was bugger-all to eat but the same old mash.

"Only a footman would write such a useless list," she said, "and leave it at a rope stall."

The young man blankly shrugged his shoulders. "I was told to leave it here for whoever to pick up, along with whatever," he said.

"What are you, an imbecile?" snapped Bette.

He looked at her. "Imbecile? Is that the same as umbilical?"

"No, that has a cord," said Bette.

"Haven't seen one of them for years," said an elderly woman passing by. "There was a time when cutting one of them was as common as cutting a toenail." She shook her head. "Not now."

"I know," sighed her equally elderly pal. "Can't remember the last one I've seen."

"Me neither," said the elderly woman. She sighed. "This place is deader than an abattoir."

"Abattoir?" said the young man. "Is that the same as an albatross?"

The elderly women looked at him. "What are you, a moron?"

"Is that the same as—" He stopped, catching a Bette Davis glare from Bette.

She sniffed. "He's been at one of those all-night barbecues."

"Not for a few nights." He sighed. "I'm starving."

"Typical," snapped the elderly woman.

Her pal tutted.

Bette watched as the women moved on to the banana stand, muttering about young men today being "wasters" and "total flatheads."

She turned to the young man. "Who gave you this?"

"A footman," he said, "in very tight trousers."

"Very tight?" said the Mae West robot, looking interested.

"Skintight, but he could pull it off," muttered the young man.

"There is only one footman that can pull off skintight," said Bette.

"Oooh," said the Mae West robot, "skintight, my favorite peeling."

"Do you ever think of anything else?" snapped Bette.

The Mae West robot blinked.

"Does everything have to be an innuendo to you?" said Bette.

"I am programmed to pun." The robot huffed. "Perhaps you should go up and see the programmer."

"Innuendo?" said the young man. "Is that the same as iguanas?"

❄

Once Bette had read the list several times, she knew she was dealing with more than a mere cleaning spree.

She was dealing with footmen changing sides.

She, Jack, and John had the goods for something spectacular, a way of breeding that could not only transform the city but elevate them to higher things, or at least get her out of trolley-pushing.

She had to be careful.

The last thing she needed was a couple of jockstrapped tossers going off half-cocked.

Clutching the so-called list, Bette, with a "this is a canteen issue," strode out of the market.

With whom to side? Was there more than one side?

The Mae West robot, sauntering at speed, followed.

Bette stopped as her Mae West robot crashed into her with a "can we do that again?" quip.

"Must you?" said Bette.

"Too much of a good thing is a wonderful—"

Bette stopped her at "thing" and, with a fair amount of tutting, headed for the canteen in the institute.

A canteen devoid of footmen and served by Mae West robots or prototypes, as the institute called them.

In fact, the cleaners, now a mere handful of three, spent most of their time in the canteen as Mae West prototypes did everything. The institute was overrun with them; so many were returned due to their "humor" not being appreciated.

There was talk of test-running robots, but who had time with all the "meat" and "fertilization" issues? Their work programs were so long that the white coats often didn't know where to start. They were so stressed that prototype massaging was not only put up with but encouraged.

A Mae West prototype, pouring tea with a "come up and see me," was always greeted with a "me first" from a white coat.

Bette pulled up a seat beside her two comrades and pushed the list across the table. "You know anything of this?"

The blonde looked at the dark one. She fingered the list. "Well, I had heard," she said.

"Heard?" said Bette, yet again cheesed off. The cleaners, just like the friggin' underground, had bypassed her. "Why didn't you say anything?"

"You're so touchy," said the blonde.

"Touchy? Me?" snapped Bette with a hard look.

"One glare from you, and I'm almost peeing myself," said the blonde.

"Don't be so ridiculous," snapped Bette as the blonde, with an "excuse me," raced to the ladies, zigzagging around several prototypes uselessly circling the canteen with trays.

"You are scary," muttered the dark one.

"*Pfff*," huffed Bette.

"Remember the underground?" said the dark one.

Bette said nothing; she had done her best to join that lot, and where did it get her? A door slammed in her face. Apparently, she was too militant.

"I am merely passionate," said Bette, watching the blonde return to her chair, "and hardworking."

"Anything worth doing is worth doing slowly," said Bette's Mae West robot.

"Some would say committed," said Bette, throwing a "shut it" look at her robot.

The dark one, with an exaggerated splutter, laughed out loud. "Well, it's not for your job; we never see you."

"You hardly raise a mop these days," chipped in the blonde. "You're always at that stupid shed."

"Come up and see us," said the Mae West robot, causing a few of her prototypes to stop circling.

The three cleaners looked at her.

"The shed—you should come and see," said Bette's Mae West robot.

"Not here," hissed Bette.

"It could change things, liberate," said Bette's Mae West robot.

"I said, not here," snapped Bette.

"Liberate?" said another prototype, mid food-ladling.

"*Pfff*, you're always on about liberation," said the blonde.

"Embryos," said the Mae West robot.

A label crashed to the floor, and a hush fell on the canteen as the prototypes stopped circling.

"We are making them," said Bette's Mae West robot.

"Shit," murmured Bette.

Chapter Twenty-One

THE SMOKING JACKET

"Manifesto the Great was a short and speedy man; foolish dreams ran from him quicker than a running tap."–The footman in tight trousers

The Mae West prototypes robots stopped, all ten of them.

"Oh, I would so love a baby," sighed one.

"Me too," said another.

"Nurturing. Wouldn't it be nice?" said a prototype behind the hot food counter.

The cleaners looked at each other; the prototypes had malfunctioned yet again.

LM-2 looked at her old comrade poised in his new 1930s American smoking jacket. She had heard he'd gone mad, but she didn't believe it. She had seen madness in James the Strong, but Manifesto the Great?

He was a man with opinions and ideas, and he was decent; she was sure of it until she saw him in that jacket.

"You like it?" said her old pal.

She didn't answer.

"The oaf of a footman gave it to me; it's all the rage in American society."

"America is on another planet," said LM-2.

He chuckled.

"And since when did you care of rages?" said LM-2.

"Oh, I'm starting it, just you wait and see; everyone will be wearing one of these soon."

"Who cares about coats?" said LM-2.

"Smoking jacket," said Manifesto the Great.

LM-2 huffed with frustration. "The city is dying around you, and you're mincing about like something in a musical?"

"Oh, we've got that all sorted," said Manifesto the Great with a smile at his reflection.

"What?" said LM-2.

"The baby thing, all sorted," he said.

LM-2 looked at him.

"The Procreation Act," said Manifesto the Great.

"You mean segregation," said LM-2.

"Well, yes, but with adjustments," said Manifesto the Great.

LM-2's face flushed with rage. "It's still segregation. I told you, you should never listen to those readers; they should be listening to you."

Manifesto the Great stopped.

He looked at his pal; he didn't have the heart to tell her it was his idea.

For nights, he had stared at the mirror, thinking how taming the city with no babies was as easy as sliding a duvet cover onto a duvet, until, that is, he saw an old Sherlock Holmes movie with hunting dogs following masters.

Then, it hit him: breeding.

The pairing up of men and women based on the talent gene.

He thought it was a grand idea.

After all, if Earth could breed a dog that rounds up sheep with a silent whistle, what could breeding do for those of the great Planet Hy Man?

"Breeding?" said LM-2. "Who is going to breed? We're as barren as gravel."

"It's all in the pairing. Sausage?" he said, tilting a plate toward her.

LM-2 looked at her old comrade poised beside his new 1930s American cocktail bar.

"You like it?" He gestured to his new bar. "It was that oaf-like footman who installed it. He's rather good with a tool; my footman can't even bend his trousers are so tight."

Manifesto the Great sipped his cocktail.

It was true, thought LM-2, *all the rumors; her old pal was as mad as a mechanical rat in heat.*

"What has happened to you? What would your mother say?" she said. "While you tuck into your sausages, the kindergartens lay empty."

"That's what my footman said." Manifesto the Great chuckled. "Before the chairman sent him packing . . . cocktail?"

Manifesto the Great, with a "bottoms up" gesture, skulled his drink, then wiped his lips with an "*arrrrh*."

"His trousers are tighter than a sausage skin," laughed Manifesto the Great.

LM-2 looked at him. Her leader was no longer leader material.

"Apparently, it's worse for the brain than head-flattening—whatever that is."

LM-2 shook her head as the oaf of a footman appeared in the doorway.

"How about that sauce, then?" he said, his large fingers clutching a jug.

Beryl watched the crowd outside swell so much that it stopped traffic. Then she realized it wasn't the crowd stopping traffic; it was what they were staring at.

With the Librarian dozing by his shelf, waiting for "feedback" from the "rebels," she sneaked out.

Creaking open the "do not open even in a fire" door, she headed into a cold, damp alley. Beryl, getting her bearings, caught a glimpse of the crowd still staring at the Building of Opulence's wall.

She slid into the crowd and was about to follow their eyes when Verruca's glum face stopped her.

Beryl, who had never played with another child, stared at "her in the orange" for a long time. She wondered about walking over, saying something about her spectacular orange outfit, until "her in the orange" stared back and poked her tongue at her, then pulled the sort of gesture Beryl had only seen her mother do.

Beryl returned the favor with a sharp finger thrusting gesture followed by her best and longest tongue-poking ever, and before she could see a reaction, "her in the orange" was pulled out of sight.

Then Beryl saw it: spray-painted, splashed in large giant-size letters, red and dripping.

"No procreation on demand."

Procreation? thought Beryl.

"Bet you it's the same nutcase who poured semen on the statues," mumbled a voice from the back.

"Pour? Semen?" said another. "How does one pour such stuff?"

"Figure of speech," said a robust-looking street cleaner.

"Semen is hardly a figure of speech," said the voice from the back.

"Sprayed like an alley rat," said the street cleaner. "All over the friggin' flowers like pickling weed killer."

Semen, thought Beryl, then stopped.

Seeds. She nodded, pulled out her pad, and wrote, "Semen? Seeds?"

A memo fluttered to the ground, followed by several more.

Bette and the two cleaners raced from the canteen, attempting to outrun the Mae West prototypes.

The last thing she wanted was those motormouths following. They were famed for spreading news like wildfire and were as in sync as the mafia, as the underground bootleggers during the 1920s prohibition. In fact, it was thought by many that they modeled themselves on said "bootleggers."

Shaking them off was as possible as brushing off a wasp. Despite ducking and diving like something out of a *Mission: Impossible* film, the prototypes stuck to the cleaners like dog shit on a shoe.

The cleaners dodged around corners, up alleyways, behind market stalls, only to turn and see the entourage still there, murmuring embryos, like comatose zombies.

Finally, Bette lost them at the banana stand.

Shoving a few ripe bananas by the prototype's feet, she heard a skid and a crash and, with a "thank the galaxies for high heels," grabbed the two dazed cleaners and ran like her life depended on it.

But still, they followed, their shoes sticky with mashed banana, until Bette saw Main Street packed like a sardine can.

She could lose an army in that crowd.

She fed her way through the crowd, a cleaner in each hand.

The prototypes stopped just shy of a little girl writing, their high heels as sticky as treacle sucking up Beryl's memos like magnets.

Bette rounded the corner into the institute's garden gate, puffing like she had just done ten rounds with a champion boxer, only to see the garden full of prototype robots and her Mae West robot giving them a guided tour.

She pushed through the milling prototype robots, made her way to the shed, and barged in without a knock.

The two cleaners and the prototype robots pushed behind, spilling into the shed like a burst dam.

They stopped just shy of the embryos, stared gobsmacked like an addict in a pharmacy. The shelves were endless, the humming of the fridge's hypnotic, the embryos so full of life.

John looked up from his Bunsen burner, Jack from his dropper poised over a Petri dish.

"What the embryonic pickle?" said John. He had no idea there were so many Mae West prototypes.

Jack grimaced, his mind counting the limitless neck massages. There were so many.

A prototype moved to touch.

"Don't—" yelled Jack.

Chapter Twenty-Two

GRAFFITI

"I only have yes-men around me who needs no men."–The chairman, stealing from the real Mae West

The chairman called a meeting; discontentment was spewing from the city like a broken sewage pipe, and they needed someone to blame.

"The women are educating themselves, refusing conjugal rights," said the chairman.

"I told you that Fanny was to be watched," said the elderly reader.

"Then feed her meat," laughed Manifesto the Great.

The chairman huffed; something was going on outside. He fingered his banana, tossed it back on the plate, and moved to the window. "What the pickle is all that noise?" he said, his hand twitching by the curtain.

The oaf of a footman entered. "Whatever you do, don't open the—"

"What?" said the chairman as the curtain flashed open.

The oaf of a footman stopped.

"Oh," said the chairman.

A voice from the back began to read. "Pro-cras-ig . . . what does it mean?"

"It's spelled wrong," snapped the elderly reader. "But the penis should give you a clue."

"That's a penis?" said the young reader.

"Of sorts," said the chairman.

"Then feed her meat," laughed Manifesto the Great.

The chairman looked at him; that wasn't such a bad idea.

He turned to the oaf of a footman. "Do those women meet somewhere, perhaps in a canteen?"

"There is an underground, sir," said the oaf of a footman.

John turned the list in his hands. "The footmen?" He shook his head. "Who'd have thought of it?"

"If they think they can save this friggin' city without me," said Bette, "they are barking up the proverbial tree. I've got the Petri dishes and the shed."

"You mean *we*," said Jack.

"That's what I said."

"Not really," muttered John.

She glared at him.

She was standing in the shed at the time with the blonde and the dark cleaner breathing down her neck.

At first, she thought it was litter on the heel of the prototype's shoes, and she was about to order them to "wipe their feet" when she looked closer.

So, it's Fanny they want, she thought. *We'll see about that!*

Fanny charged into her underground office, slammed the door shut, and caught her breath.

"Open," she shouted.

The drawers jumped into action; files flew up in the air.

She fumbled with her backpack, looked up, and, through the haze of papers, caught sight of LM-2 and Maisie staring at her like teachers handing out detention.

"That was helpful," said LM-2.

"What?" said Fanny, still panting.

"Juvenile," said Maisie.

"Don't know what you're talking about," said Fanny, feigning innocence.

The two women stared at Fanny's "a robot is not just for birthdays" backpack.

"Thought you were in talks with the footmen," said Fanny, attempting a casual toss of her backpack.

The bag, missing the drawer, clattered to the ground.

A spray can rolled out.

Another followed.

Red paint oozed with a hiss.

"Here's me offering up our underground like it was the height of intelligence," said LM-2. "And you're spraying penises everywhere like a teenager."

"And it's clear you've not seen one of them for a while," said Maisie.

"How can anyone take us seriously when you can't even spell procreation properly?" snapped LM-2.

Fanny shifted uncomfortably. "Uprising calls for drastic measures?"

"There I was, talking about the evils of segregation in front of a footman wearing trousers so tight that I could see the label on his underpants." LM-2 stopped and caught her breath. "Then, that oaf of a footman appeared, pulled the curtains to reveal—" She stopped.

"An apparition that had the other footmen making foreskin jokes," snapped Maisie.

"It's not easy looking like you know what you're talking about in the face of 'man' jokes," said LM-2.

"And as for that sperm—" Maisie shook her head.

Fanny fumbled with the top of the can. "Yes. Well, I ran out of paint."

The can hissed again. Fanny wrestled with the lid, and red paint squirted everywhere.

"Pickling cans," mumbled Fanny. She looked up at the two women, arms crossed. "I mean, who invented these friggin' lids?"

"Well, you've set things in motion," said LM-2.

"Good," said Fanny, with a vigorous finger-wiping.

"The cleaners are against us, thanks to you," said Maisie.

"But I was in disguise," said Fanny.

"Not so your daughter," said Maisie. "Everyone saw the girl in orange and, well, put two and two together."

Fanny, cursing her daughter's flamboyant love of color, blushed.

The two women stared at her.

"As I said, uprising calls for drastic measures."

Beryl headed back to the library, racing in to find the Librarian shifting uncomfortably, chained to his shelf. It was not his greatest plan.

No one seemed to care.

He thought it would jolt the leader, but all he did was come in and wave a burger under his nose, waffling on about "iron and strength."

"What's procreation when it's at home?" said Beryl, loosening his handcuffs. "And what's it got to do with seeds?"

"I'll tell you later," said the Librarian, rubbing his wrists.

"And what is that?" she said, ripping the curtain open.

The Librarian glared at the giant apparition with a ball and chain attached to what looked like a poor attempt at foreskin. The whole thing was completely out of proportion.

"Well, that," he said, "is a drawing done by a woman who has not seen one for quite some time. Perhaps with a mild vision impairment."

He coughed.

"Send for Manifesto the Great's footman. The one in the tight trousers."

Fanny grabbed her binoculars and stared at the street. She could see a posse of men looking at a large map like builders at a building site.

She stared closer. It wasn't a map at all. She refocused her binoculars. It was a spreadsheet.

"That list of out-of-date women," said Fanny with restrained panic. "Is it operational?"

"Operational? It's what sparked the Librarian's sit-in," said Maisie.

"Oh," said Fanny.

The men began point her way . . . towards her basement.

"Bugger," muttered Fanny.

She turned to LM-2. "Does anyone know we're here?"

"Just about every woman in the city."

"Bollocks," said Fanny.

"Well, you did want to be inclusive," said LM-2.

Fanny, panic rising in her like a bad curry, watched as several grim-faced cleaners armed with ladders and buckets appeared from behind the posse.

She could see they were arguing with the men and that militant so-and-so of a cleaner pointing toward her basement.

"Shit," said Fanny.

"We did warn you of the kiss and tell," said Maisie.

The men began to march toward her basement.

"We need to move," panicked Fanny.

"What? And leave all this mess?" said LM-2.

"Open," shouted Fanny.

Drawers flew open; more files filled the air then crashed to the floor.

LM-2, on the verge of throwing a wobbly, snapped. "Will you stop with the dreaded word?"

Fanny screeched, "Open now!"

The cabinet inched open like a door.

The posse began to knock on the door.

"Quickly—through there." Fanny gestured to the doorway.

The posse pushed against the door, now wedged shut by a knee-high pile of files.

Fanny pushed Maisie and LM-2 into the dark passageway, barking "shut" at the filing cabinet.

The filing cabinet clicked shut, and Fanny flicked on a torch.

"Quick," she said. "Time is of the . . . how do you put it?"

"Essence," said Maisie.

Chapter Twenty-Three

TUNNELS AND PETTICOATS

"Soon, bed-diving, like fishing, barbecuing, and a good old-fashioned chase-the-chicken-around-the-field, was off the table."—Manifesto the Great

It was a dark passageway that Fanny assumed no one knew of but a few of her key women and her.

How wrong was she?

Racing down the tunnel with LM-2 and Maisie at her rear, the last thing she expected to bump into was a very handsome footman. Fanny clambered into his chest; caught off guard, she looked up into his face like a startled chicken.

She had never seen a footman with such a way with trousers before; in fact, she had no experience with any footman. She was used to her Mae West robot getting in the way. Soon she was putting on the sort of coquettish behavior that had LM-2 gagging and Maisie fuming.

Manifesto the Great's footman greeted them like he was expecting them, like he was all part of their plan; not that they had one.

He said he was taking them to meet the Librarian, who was boasting of a proposal, "a scheme to beat all schemes."

"So I've heard," snapped LM-2.

"He's changed sides," said Manifesto the Great's footman.

"So you said," said LM-2. She turned to Fanny and stopped.

Fanny, trouser-struck, was drinking in every word of Manifesto the

Great's footman like he was the Second Coming. Then, when he pulled a hand-size map from the crotch of his trouser, she nearly fainted.

"Pull yourself together," snapped Maisie. "He's a man."

"It's the trousers," she sighed.

Manifesto the Great's footman, with a rustle of his map, talked of plans. "And he wants you to implement it," he said to Fanny.

She blinked. "Me?"

Manifesto the Great's footman nodded. His manicured finger pointed to the exits and entrances of the Building of Opulence, the new library, the old library, the room with a view, the canteens for the workers, the "canteen for the readers," and the newsroom, which, according to him, was a "beehive of men watching everything from Earth to the sewage plant on state-of-the-art mirrors."

Fanny stared at the map, mesmerized.

"Nothing gets past those mirrors; that building is as transparent as a nylon petticoat."

Fanny nodded; she knew all about petticoats.

Maisie nudged her.

"It's like a maze," said Manifesto the Great's footman. "One could get lost for days."

LM-2 rolled her eyes. She'd spent her whole life there. What was she, blind?

"I *have* been there," she snapped.

"But never incognito," said Manifesto the Great's footman. "A whole new ballgame."

Fanny, confused, barely listened. *Why me?*

Maisie, red-faced with frustration, pulled Fanny close to her. "Focus," she hissed.

"We are walking into a cesspit of backstabbers," said LM-2. "He's probably one of them. I've seen the shape of our leader, and it's not a pretty sight."

Manifesto the Great's footman blushed; guilt flashed across his face. "I had no idea about the cocktails," he said.

"So you say," said LM-2.

"But I have my suspicions," he said.

"We need more than suspicions," said LM-2. "We need to know who is for and who is against."

"Well, he can come against me any day," said a robotic voice from nowhere.

The women stopped.

"Who the Petri dish is that?" said Maisie.

Bette appeared from the shadows.

Before she could say anything, let alone throw her famous Bette Davis glare, she juddered, overbalanced by her Mae West robot and the entourage of prototypes colliding into her back, the braking mechanism of a prototype being on par with a bald tire on ice.

"Will you stop with the shoving?" Bette pushed back.

The prototypes clattered to a halt.

"That's the leader's footman," hissed one.

"The cocktail footman?" said another.

"He can fix me a cocktail anytime," said a third, followed by a monotone, "Ha, ha, ha."

"Look, I said I had no idea about the cocktails," snapped Manifesto the Great's footman.

Fanny, Manifesto the Great's footman's tight trousers forgotten, eyeballed the tiny cleaner.

Bette adjusted her stance.

"Bette," hissed Fanny.

"Fanny," Bette hissed back.

The two stared at each other like alley cats ready to strike.

"Who are you?" said Manifesto the Great's footman.

"She's a pushy upstart," huffed Fanny.

"There is nothing upstart about me," hissed Bette.

"You're from the institute," said Maisie.

"We're the cleaners," said the blonde and the dark cleaners, gesturing to their aprons like credentials.

"She's got embryos," said a prototype.

"Shut it," said Bette.

"Haven't we all," muttered Fanny.

"But hers are in a minibar," said another prototype.

"Minibar?" Maisie looked at LM-2.

"I said shut it," snapped Bette.

Maisie and LM-2 eyed Bette's entourage, filling the tunnel like an army.

"What would you know about a minibar?" said Maisie.

"Plenty," said Bette.

"*Pfff*, as if," said Fanny.

"Look," said Bette, "I have something way beyond anything you can imagine, something that will blow this segregation to smithereens, but I'm not gonna tell you in a dark tunnel with some ponce in a tight pair of trousers."

"Ma'am," said Manifesto the Great's footman, "the budget of one's uniform is of limited resources."

Ignoring Manifesto the Great's footman, Bette eyed her opposition. "You're better off with me than against."

Manifesto the Great's footman nodded, then headed down the tunnel. The others followed, apart from Fanny.

He stopped and turned.

"Let's go," he yelled. "That Librarian ain't getting any younger."

The chairman entered the room with a view. He was about to let rip. How could they possibly let her, a woman old enough to be, well, catchable, slip away? What were his men, pussies?

He stared at the useless bunch of readers; they had no idea. The only thing they were interested in was the next sauce to dip their barbecued bananas in.

"We have a revolt brewing; women are slipping through our fingers, disappearing from rooms, and—" He looked at the oaf of a footman. "And footmen. Cleaners are joining them."

"Cleaners?" said a young reader.

"Sort of like a prototype," said a reader.

"But without the massages," said another.

"They are women!" shouted the chairman. "And as manipulable as a pot of clay. If we don't do something—" He stopped, as Manifesto the Great's voice could be heard from the corridor.

He had the voice of his father.

"What about a speech?" he said. "He can still read, can't he?"

Chapter Twenty-Four

WIELDING AND MOPS

"An obelisk does not live up to its complicated spelling."–Fanny

The Librarian, unchained by an old shelf full of has-been memoirs, rubbed his wrists. He eyed his new larger-than-expected tribe and was on the verge of feeling smug when Bette and Fanny began the sort of carry-on that had the others uncomfortably transfixed.

"We meet at last," he said, not quite sure where to direct his gaze.

No one heard.

Fanny was talking of Bette wielding her mop as she had "never wielded before," and Bette was having none of it.

She eyed the so-called rebel, a woman with an expensive haircut, the glossy skin of pampered creams, and an underwire that even a schoolboy would not believe, and told her where she could shove her mop, causing a few to wince.

"There is nothing wrong with my wielding," she snapped.

"It has no passion," said Fanny.

"Passion? You try wielding a mop and a trolly under the hum of disinfectant and see how long passion lasts."

"I quite like disinfectant," muttered the blonde cleaner.

The Librarian, trying to inject some sort of authority, yelled, "There'll be no wielding of mops."

Bette carried on. "You're an arsehole."

"What was that?" said Fanny.

"You heard," said Bette. "I knew it the moment I first saw you, when you slammed the door in my face. 'Too friggin' militant,' you said. Well, I'll give you militant."

Fanny blushed; it was all coming back to her. "There was so much kiss-and-tell back then," she mumbled. "So hard to know who's who."

"Yeah, right. You saw a cleaner," said Bette.

"And you are a bit scary," said LM-2.

"Me?" Bette looked to her comrades.

They nodded.

"You are a bit," said the dark cleaner.

"More than a bit," said the blonde cleaner. "They call you 'she who must be avoided.'"

"Who?" said Bette.

"The other cleaners, and those are the polite ones."

In the end, it was the bending of Manifesto the Great's footman that silenced the row.

Grunting over a whiteboard stuffed in a corner, he ripped his trousers with a grunt, causing accusations to turn to laughter.

He looked up, red-faced, hitching the large whiteboard into position, not factoring in the Librarian's wig perched on his head like a tea cozy.

The women stared as the wig flew across the room like a flattened seagull, landing on the corner of an unfinished model of an obelisk.

Fanny stared at his wig, perched like a drunk on a pushbike, and wondered how long before it would plop.

The Librarian, catching her look, jumped in to lay out his plan, which was pretty simple.

"A mere overrunning of the room with a view should do it," he said.

"Mere?" said LM-2, trying not to stare at his bald head.

"With cocktails," mumbled Manifesto the Great's footman.

"Cocktails?" said Fanny. "We are using cocktails?"

"Exactly," sighed Manifesto the Great.

"Well, of course. How else do you expect us to overthrow a bunch of men?" said the Librarian. "With Mae West prototypes?"

The prototypes began to jostle.

"There is more to us than high heels," said one.

"I was thinking more along the lines of something with integrity, something women of the future could remember." Fanny blushed. "After my death."

"This is not about you," snapped Bette.

"Much larger," said the Mae West robot.

"The survival of our planet," came a monotone voice from the back.

"But something heroic wouldn't go amiss," said Fanny.

"Being a heroine is not all beer and Skittles," said Bette. "We all must make sacrifices."

"Here, here," chorused the prototypes.

"It's *hero*," snapped Fanny, "not *heroine*, and I am aware of the Skittle issue." She huffed. "I just thought a statue would be nice; perhaps an obelisk?"

"An obelisk for a graffiti artist who can't spell?" said Bette.

"I ran out of paint," said Fanny.

"An obelisk is something four-legged creatures lift their leg to pee on," said the blonde cleaner.

"Not a flower in sight," said the dark cleaner. "Not like Manifesto the Great's statue."

Fanny stopped. "The leader has a statue?"

"Don't they all?" muttered Maisie.

"But he's an imbecile, flatheaded to a pancake level," said Fanny.

"And it's covered in flowers," said the dark cleaner.

"I've busted my innards for this city, and do you see me complaining, wanting a friggin' obelisk?" snapped the Librarian.

"We're getting off track here," said LM-2.

"I couldn't give a flying Petri dish," he lied, and he was about to say more when his wig plopped to the ground, revealing his name scrawled across the unfinished obelisk.

Fanny looked out of the window, catching sight of a cluster of overflowing bins. Someone, probably artistic and definitely fed up waiting for the bin emptier, had created a statue out of the rubbish.

A head out of "tastes like steak" packets, a torso out of empty soya boxes, and what looked like a way better appendage than her graffiti out of used hemp stubs.

It was an inspiring feat, more so when circling about the bottom were several fat mechanical rats unable to access any food. One hissed, the other reared up on its hind legs and made to swipe, neither noticing as a sleek rat scaled the construction like a mountaineer, as fast as a ferret.

"I take it the leader's statue is in the usual place?" she said.

No one answered. Manifesto the Great's footman was giving his "we are all heroes" speech.

"Us men and women need to stick together," he said, rubbing the prototypes the wrong way.

"And what are we, chopped Teflon?" said one.

"Yeah," said another.

Fanny watched as the sleek rat clambered to the top of the pile.

The other rats tried to follow.

"You're an integral part in the uprising and more," said Manifesto the Great's footmen to the prototypes.

The ferret-like rat pelted pellets of hardened soya at his enemies.

Fanny wondered, an idea forming.

"You are the Vegas nerve of the revolution," said a deep voice.

The crowd hushed; Fanny turned to see the oaf of a footman's vast expanse filling the doorway.

No one noticed his lopsided grin.

It was but a simple plan set up on a whiteboard with many diagrams made and rubbed off.

The Librarian, not great with a whiteboard, allowed the oaf of a footman to do "the honors" despite Manifesto the Great's footman's "I don't trust that grin" reservations.

The rebels were too excited.

The Librarian made it sound so easy.

"With my motorized wheelchair, it will be a cinch," he said.

The prototypes clapped their hands with glee. The thought of overthrowing the room with a view, not to mention tying up the readers, had the prototypes almost wetting themselves.

"I'll bring the rope," said one.

"Me too," said another.

Another appeared from nowhere, clutching tape, masks, and a selection of handcuffs.

"A good woman is always prepared," she said.

"For what?" said Manifesto the Great's footman.

"Well, for anything," said Bette's Mae West robot. "I have some lubricant."

Silence.

"For massages," said Bette's Mae West robot.

"They won't know what hit them," said an almost hysterical prototype. "Before they've even had time to adjust their wigs, we'll have them tied, masked, and muted." She looked at Bette's Mae West robot. "And massaged into submission."

"And what if the worst happens?" said LM-2.

"Worst?" said Bette. "There is no *worst*; we have all the cards. You have me, the shed, plus the two white coats."

"Petri dishes and embryos," sighed a prototype.

Fanny, already angry enough to punch her pint-size rival in the face, raged as Bette told of her fertilizing shed. This uncouth loudmouth mop-wielder was going to do what she had dreamed of for years: liberate women while saving the friggin' planet.

Fanny's jealousy burned like the furnace of a speeding steam engine. Her ideas of weapons of mass destruction were now as stupid as the Librarian's obelisk.

She had to do something, but what?

"The thing is to look natural," said Manifesto the Great's footman.

"Absolutely," said Bette.

"Totally," said the cleaners as the prototypes clicked their high heels to attention.

No one noticed as the oaf-like footman, with his lopsided grin expanding into a devilish sneer, left without a word.

Apart from the Librarian.

Chapter Twenty-Five

STATUES AND THIGHS

"They can lead us to the kitchen, but they'll never make us swallow."–Fanny

The courtyard of greatness had expanded over the years, with dozens of male statues lining its pathways. Statues of men like Greek gods inspired by Wife-ie's hubby, "the grand-daddy of Planet Hy Man," and James the Strong's massive image.

Hubby's statue, with a fork in one hand and a diary in the other, still held up the old library even though the Building of Opulence had engulfed it.

While James the Strong's gigantic illuminations flashed nightly onto the glass entrance of the Building of Opulence, his large thighs astride the double doors like he was about to squat. For many, it broke the mold, causing a craze of squatting holograms in the city streets and just as many transporter accidents.

The sudden flashing of a gigantic man can do that to a driver, and after one too many collisions, holograms were banned, except in the courtyard of greatness.

For years, a young and sane Manifesto the Great walked past the large images of his forebearers. Staring at his father's massive thighs, Hubble's fork propping up the old library stirred jealousy in his loins. He longed for something bigger, better, and way more poignant.

Fueled by arguments about flesh-eating with his mother and his humor still intact, he designed his statue: he, astride a four-legged creature like Atilla the Hun, with a dozen more creatures behind.

If his mother saw it, she never let on.

It was a magnificent sight, so large that picnics were held on it until a "so-called" accident with a flask left a stain in the worst possible place.

But by then, Manifesto the Great, head flattened but happy, had no idea who Atilla the Hun was, let alone about incontinence.

The chairman, a man with excellent domination skills and a brilliant imagination, often stared at the stain, marveling at its ability to withstand all weather.

However, thanks to the oaf of a footman's latest information, stains were the last thing on his mind.

He watched as an eagle-like mechanical bird fluttered onto Manifesto the Great's hat, its large frame dwarfed by the giant sombrero.

More birds followed.

The chairman turned to the oaf of a footman. "Are you sure of your facts?"

"Yes, sir," said the oaf a footman.

"The cleaners too?" said the chairman.

The oaf of footman nodded.

The chairman watched as a bird dropping spilled onto the rim.

"What is the use of spying if you don't know what to do with the info?" said the chairman.

"The men are ready," said the oaf of a footman.

"Footmen are hardly men," said the chairman.

"And that is hardly a creature," said the oaf of a footman. "Nothing is that large; you could perform a speech on that thing and still have room for a tea party."

The chairman stopped as an idea hit him as quickly as the plopping of a bird dropping.

Why not hold speeches here? Being surrounded by statues would surely intimidate and suppress; of course, we'd need a balcony.

"Is the balcony moveable?" he said. "By the room with a view?"

The oaf of a footman looked as his hopefully new leader, and as the footman uttered an "I guess so," the chairman began pontificating of traps, polished floors, and keeping the health and safety out of things.

"Let's erect the speech gallery here," he said, "with a sound system that fills the streets and a speech that promises the impossible."

"Speech?" said the footman. "Bit of a tall order for the leader."

"Don't worry about him," said the chairman. He looked at the oaf of a footman. "Have you heard of dubbing?"

The oaf of a footman caught on with a smile. "It is but my forte, sir," he said.

"Good." The chairman sighed. "And we'll leave a nice slippery floor and a great big gap to welcome the so-called rebels with."

"On the speech gallery?" said the oaf of a footman.

"No!" snapped the chairman. "The room with a view."

The oaf a footman nodded. He hadn't a clue what he was on about.

It all started with a mop and the clatter of a trolley.

Bette, taking charge, shoved her Mae West robot and the prototypes into the cleaning cupboard while the blonde and the dark cleaner were on "standby" by the watercooler with orders to "look casual."

Manifesto the Great's footman, along with his comrades armed with anything they could get their hands on and hide in their trousers, were outside "keeping watch."

The chairman did wonder as he passed by a particularly young footman sporting the sort of bulge that even a male ballet dancer would not get away with. Poised with a question about appropriate fitting, he was stopped short as a clatter burst from outside the room with a view.

The readers, bundled in jackets, jumped. "What was that?"

They were sitting around the table in the room with a view, mid refurbishing.

They heard another crash.

Manifesto the Great, skidding across the floor with his refilled beverage, grabbed at a chair and caught his balance, spilling half his caffeine.

The floor, polished to the max, was as slippery as ice.

"Mind," snapped a reader.

The leader caught his breath and glared at the oaf of a footman.

Manifesto the Great's footman, clocking the spillage, skidded across to mop up.

"Was it absolutely necessary to polish the floor?" said the leader. He gestured at the Teflon covering where the patio windows once were, sparking a stagger. "With all this going on?"

"Mind," shouted a voice from the back.

"All will become clear," said the oaf of a footman.

"Clear? What do you mean, clear?" said the elderly reader. "Some-one'll break their neck on that floor."

"Did you not wear the slippers as suggested?" said the oaf of a footman.

"Slippers? Who the pickle wears slippers to a meeting?" said the elderly reader.

The oaf of a footman eyed the elder reader's polished shoes. "Yes, well, whatever you do, don't get up until I give you the nod."

Packed like sardines, limbs bunched up between trolleys and hoovers, it hadn't taken long for the prototypes to grumble.

Even the Mae West robot was not happy.

Perching by cleaning fluid has as much to do with massage, as, well, a hoover. As the handle of one was making itself known near her seating equipment, she grabbed it, wrenching the handle from the body.

The prototypes, assuming she was making a weapon, followed suit, and soon, armed like fetish cleaners that'd have even Mae West blushing, they broke free. Anticipation, it seemed, caused a malfunction in the wiring.

Brandishing enough lubricants to grease up an army of tanks, they made for the door.

The Librarian, with way too much faith in his wheelchair, tried to round them off, but the prototypes were as unstoppable as a herd of wildebeests.

Manifesto the Great, hearing the commotion, skidded to the door, burst it open with a clatter, filled his tiny lungs with air, and yelled, "What the spermicide is going on? I have a speech to prepare." And toppled to the floor.

Fanny, poised by the cleaning cupboard, stopped. Speech! Why, of course.

She grabbed Maisie and LM-2 and, with a "come with me," headed to the bowels of the old library, where the stationary was limitless.

Fanny slid into the "dark" room of the library, unaware of Beryl's presence.

"We need a banner," she said to her comrades. "And leaflets."

"The cleaners will be up in arms," hissed Masie. "Leaflets make more mess than your graffiti."

"*Pfff*," said Fanny, "those bozos are too busy sucking up to the footmen to notice."

Maisie and LM-2 looked at each other. Had she always been this crazy?

They didn't stay long; their idea of a revolution had nothing to do with banners and leaflets and more to do with the promise of Petri dishes. If there was to be breeding in the city, then a banner was hardly going to change things, and as for leaflets, what were they going to do but clutter up the street?

Beryl watched as Maisie and LM-2 deserted their comrade.

She watched as Fanny rustled in the dark and offered to help.

Fanny turned to see a slip of a girl the same age as her daughter; she smiled, touched her hair.

"Call me Fanny," she said.

Making a banner was a piece of piss for Beryl, and as for leaflets, she could print them off as quick as tying up the Librarian. Within an hour, they had a banner large enough to be seen in space and enough leaflets to keep the cleaners busy for weeks.

Fanny blew on the ink, then stood up from her banner with a satisfied "finished."

Beryl, mid leaflet folding, glanced at the large, perfectly spelled "foreplay or no play" and was wise enough not to ask what it meant.

Chapter Twenty-Six

THE COURTYARD OF GREATNESS

"Some would say foreplay has little to do with play; others would disagree."–Reader

Manifesto the Great stuffed into a transporter with a plate of sausages was whisked away to the courtyard of greatness to "christen" the new speech balcony with a speech.

A courtyard so large you could park the three has-been spaceships and a fleet of transporters and still have room for a dance.

How could he perform on an empty stomach to such a crowd?

He stepped out of his transport limo with indigestion, the oaf of a footman, and no idea what was hidden beneath the speech balcony.

No one did.

No one had a clue of Fanny perched incognito—apart, that is, from Beryl.

The Librarian was in panic mode. His carefully planned "it will be a doddle" coup was crumbling quicker than a cream cracker.

He thought on his proverbial. "Where the pickling hell are those cleaners?" he hissed.

"Cleaners?" said the chairman.

"Why, yes," said the Librarian. "We have an issue with cobwebs."

"Cobwebs? I thought they died along with the last spider," said the chairman.

The Librarian stuttered for an answer.

"Cocktail?" said Manifesto the Great's footman, appearing from behind the chairman with a tray.

The prototypes grabbed their chance. Spurred on by the need to massage, they poured into the room with a view, bustling like a brood of hens.

The clipping of high heels was so overpowering that the chairman had to yell like a referee. No one heard or cared.

The readers, downing their finger food, knew the best was yet to come; the prototypes hadn't factored in the polished floor.

Fanny, with her banner and her leaflets stuffed in her backpack, headed for the courtyard of greatness. Her head was buzzing with conversation and arguments; she had learned a lot from her mistakes, and this time, it was going to be different.

With her incognito technique perfected, she would show them all and make that bozo Bette eat her words.

Manifesto the Great climbed the new speech balcony, wondering about a wave.

The oaf of a footman, brushing imaginary fluff from the leader's jacket, told him to "reassure the masses and talk like your father."

Manifesto the Great jumped onto his box and stared out into the crowd.

The oaf of a footman slid behind and pulled out the "dubbing" equipment.

Manifesto the Great pulled out his speech.

The oaf of a footman, poised by the "play" button, watched and waited.

He was the last to see, and by then, it was too late.

Fanny had spent all morning in the courtyard of greatness attaching her banner. Once finished, she climbed to the top of Manifesto the Great's statue and perched under the brim of his hat.

Before he even had a chance to say, "Friends, citizens, and workers," Fanny had released her "foreplay or no play" banner.

The banner, attached to the various appendages of Manifesto the Great and his four-legged creatures via an elegant system of ropes and pulleys, unfolded like a concertina flag, showering a sea of leaflets onto the crowd.

It could have been a showstopper, but she took it too far.

The crowd gasped.

Manifesto the Great stopped.

"Go on," hissed the oaf of a footman, deaf to the crowd's "oohs" and "aahs."

The leader gestured.

The crowd began to cheer; some applauded.

The oaf of a footman looked up.

"Foreplay" plopped open.

The crowd stopped; some muttered.

The "foreplay" confused many; it had been so long that many thought it was illegal.

"What the ectoplasm" echoed through the dubbing system.

Fanny watched as the chairman arrived like royalty, his smile freezing as he caught sight of the banner.

Fanny pulled her bra from her shoulders. Using it as a slingshot, she began to pummel the leader with hard-as-nails hemp balls and soya effluent.

The crowd cheered themselves hoarse as the two men hopped and skipped from the pellets.

Until, that is, they caught sight of the Librarian.

While Fanny was stopping traffic and more with her banners and talk of mass destruction, the Librarian, hell-bent on controlling Bette's Mae West robot and the prototypes, was circling with little effect.

Chasing them was not easy in a wheelchair, especially with a squad of footmen and cleaners behind, making reversing impossible, and as for "cornering," they may as well have strapped an anchor to his wheels.

Until, that is, he hit the polished floor.

Bette's Mae West robot, her hand oozing massage oil, went for the elderly reader with a "get him." He, being the only reader to hate massages with a passion, claiming they were as soothing as a dose of laxatives, surprised everyone with a spritely jump from his chair.

He skidded. "Shit!"

"Mind," yelled someone.

"Careful," yelled another.

The Mae West robot continued like a torpedo set on its target. Rubbing her hands like a Russian shot-putter ready to throw, she slid across the floor, lubricant dripping like invisible treacle.

The prototypes followed, their heels clipping and skidding.

The elderly reader made a move; his feet gave way, he grabbed at the table, and bananas, peaches, and grapes crashed to his feet.

Stopping on an ice rink would have been easier.

The elderly reader attempted to stand and skidded on a banana.

A few winced.

The Mae West robot, with a speed not programmed to control, headed straight for the Teflon.

The prototypes followed.

The Librarian sped past the elderly reader.

The elderly reader's trousers caught in the wheel.

"Shit."

The Mae West robot stalled, just shy of the Teflon.

It flapped in her face.

The Librarian grabbed her.

The prototypes stopped.

The Teflon blew open, revealing the sort of drop that would make a stomach sink.

"Whew," uttered someone.

The Mae West robot spluttered, her circuits bursting into action.

She skidded into the Teflon and beyond.

The Librarian clutched at a curtain.

It ripped.

The elderly reader made for the window frame and missed, disappearing through the Teflon attached to a man he hated as much as massaging, and for the first time in his life, he knew what it was like to "fly by the seat of his pants."

The prototypes followed like lemmings.

Fanny, boldly parading around the rim of Manifesto the Great's giant sombrero, was on the cusp of her weapons-of-mass-destruction speech.

"How long can a woman go on being denied a sausage?" she yelled and was about to say more until she clapped eyes on the Librarian soaring through the air, his wheelchair not far behind.

Fanny, caught off-guard, skidded on a leaflet, tripped over the corner of her banner, and plummeted to the ground.

The crowd circled her broken body, still clutching the "P" of her banner.

"They can lead us to the kitchen, but they'll never make us swallow," murmured Fanny before her eyes fluttered shut.

The Librarian's end was worse; he didn't even have time to cough, let alone splutter.

The readers gathered about the Teflon, gingerly peering behind and watched as the Librarian, free for the first time in decades from his wheelchair, made like a skydiver.

"Extra fruit; nice touch," whispered the chairman to the oaf of a footman. "Even I didn't see that coming."

The oaf of a footman said nothing; the extra fruit was the leader's idea.

After the fall of Fanny and the Librarian, the chairman ordered the catching of the turtles.

"They are the glue that held this so-called coup together," he said, and no one argued.

Most city folk, fed up with them stomping on gardens and roaring in the middle of the night, were glad to see the back of them.

The turtles were lassoed and dismembered quicker than a car in a scrapyard. The institute, completely focused on the breeding of babies, shoved the parts into a skip, pending a good sort.

The underground, trying to save some of the turtles, led them to the outlands, and they almost made it but were followed.

A fight broke out, leading to the spilling of oils and the blackening of the lands—a fight that no one in the city knew of.

The fight did go down in the hippie colony's annuals but was never mentioned in the fieldworkers' storytelling.

Losing is not something they liked to remember, let alone talk of around the campfire.

It was the final splitting of the two groups; the hippies not helping was a sore point.

As the last turtle was led away by the men, LM-2 became the first outlaw and disappeared. It was rumored that she had joined the hippie colony, helping to camouflage their wind machines as scarecrows.

Ten years later

"Bonding," the Librarian had told her, was "where the real power lies. Make a tribe and before you know it, you have a group who will lay down their life for you."
In the end, it was the hoover the women laid down for Beryl . . .

Chapter Twenty-Seven

LIPSTICKS AND WIGS

"At the end, there was Beryl."–Verruca

Beryl looked in the mirror; she was nothing like her mother. She didn't wear lipstick and wore her hair short, but now, at twenty, she realized if she didn't do something, the only thing that set her apart from her father was a pair of breasts.

She lived with the constant "oh, you're so like him." A comment that had her gazing at his picture with a screwed-up "really?" expression.

He had the look of a man who hardly laughed and scolded those who did—nothing like the inventor of spying equipment. But then, as she suspected, it was all fluff and talk; after all, his memoirs were but a three-minute read full of diagrams as easy to understand as a bra clip.

Beryl had the smarts of a savvy prostitute. Not only had she mastered filing, fetching without flustering, and looking like listening when not, but she had become good at getting others to do for her—commanding, as her father called it.

She had seen the rise, fall, and brushing under the carpet of Fanny, the Librarian, and the cleaners. She knew what not to do, shutting up when it came to her mother being number one.

A mother who ran a speakeasy.

A mother not great with women.

A mother from the right side of the tracks who threw it all away, who serviced readers for a penny and enjoyed it way too much.

Who, choking on a macaroon, passed away, her red lipstick perfect, and little to say apart from the temperature of her caffeine.

Beryl had heard it all, and she knew the truth: her mother was as fond of macaroons as she was of cold caffeine.

"Ignore them," the Librarian used to tell her. "That's what I've done all my life, and look where it has gotten me."

Beryl stared at her reflection. The last time she saw the Librarian, he was out of it, splattered on the pavement like a squashed starfish, his battered wheelchair feet away, upturned, the wheels spinning uselessly.

Hardly obelisk material.

It had taken her a while to adjust to "no" Librarian, to adapt to the chairman's ways, know how far to push. Their relationship was a pleasurable tussle of wills for him and an endless learning process for her.

It's time to move on, she thought, *or at least get a new look.*

She tried on a Cleopatra-style wig—one of the Librarian's favorites, inspired from the flapper years on earth.

She screwed up her face; it was worse than her haircut.

She walked into the Librarian's secret cupboard and stared at the array of hidden wigs and books.

Perhaps something with height, she thought. *Something to shock, but not too much.*

She eyed her reflection, sliding on one wig after another, and told herself that she would win where Fanny had failed.

Serval hours later, the new Beryl was in the basement sorting rejects, devices destined for the big scrapheap in the sky.

The basement had not always been the basement. Before the "fall of the underground," it was the old library, her home. Now it was her workplace full of shelves crammed with debunked parts of Mae West prototypes, their microchips pulled and binned alongside with the turtle designs and, well, anything else to do with Fanny's underground era.

An era washed from history, and it was Beryl's job to see that it stayed that way.

It had taken years to collect all the pieces and even more to work out how to "defunct" a Mae West prototype.

Years because the institute was busy coordinating the making of babies.

Beryl, grimly crossing out her "done" on the whiteboard, stopped, counted the devices at her feet, then continued her crossing off.

Jack and John appeared, arms full of boxes jam-packed with devices and leads.

Jack and John, who had dreamed of white coats and drinking "top-notch" caffeine, had no idea that in the end, they would be in a basement helping women like Beryl. They thought they'd be heading the whole baby-making process; they were as much at the head of things as a cleaner. In fact, they may as well have been cleaners. All they did was shuffle piles of unwanted equipment from A to B and often back again.

They stopped.

Was that Beryl? In a wig? They stared at her new beehive look, blonde, with bows.

"Beryl?" said John.

She turned with a curt "hello" smile and then returned to her "done" crossing off.

"The chairman will be pleased," said John with a glum expression.

"Yes," said Jack, "not a trace left."

He sighed; he quite liked the Mae West robot.

John eyed Beryl's hair and was about to make a "new look" comment when he caught a flash of a glare, something she had taken to lately—a take on Bette's glare, yet with more authority.

It was just a flash, nothing more, yet . . .

If they knew where that look would lead, they would have tossed Beryl to the outlands like a spent toilet roll.

✳

While Beryl hid things in the basement, the city adjusted to test-tube babies.

The problem was the babies were females, and like the Alien women, they were built like Amazonian warriors, strong enough to lift a forklift with one finger but, funny enough, infertile.

The men thought once they got the whole egg-in-a-Petri-dish thing sorted, life would be easy, and bed-diving for fun, a given.

The truth was, many women would rather a root canal treatment than a roll in the hay with their partner, some even screwing up their nose at a peck on the cheek, and the men were not only fed up but growing disheartened.

It seemed that the women were rising again, and the last thing the chairman needed was an upstart like Beryl in the wrong place.

She had a look about her that reminded him of Fanny, Bette, and the others who almost toppled the city, who took him by surprise, and he had heard that she had been visiting the institute.

She needed to be snubbed out like a hemp fag, and he knew just how to do it.

Chapter Twenty-Eight

WHITEBOARD

"Sperm gave men the ability to lift, yell, and make things rise, while ovaries made women cry at the oddest of things and burn toast."–The Librarian

Beryl, her beehive wig back in its box, walked into the room with a view; it was as empty as the whiteboard Manifesto the Great was now staring at.

He didn't look up.

She clattered a tray onto the table.

Nothing, even when his footman entered and the chairman behind him.

The leader was as still as a statue; not even a hair twitched.

Manifesto the Great, when thinking, didn't hear; thinking took up all his powers but never led to much.

Not that anyone said anything or questioned his leadership, even though he repeated himself, fluffed his speeches, and was frequently found at the market looking for the way home.

The status quo suited them, and the men had never had it so good.

Beryl looked at Manifesto the Great's footman, now seriously old and still in tight trousers, the sort covered in darning spots from splitting when bending. He was now so old that bending was a distant memory, like his good looks, but his loyalty to something better for the city remained.

He mouthed a "wait."

Beryl picked up a marker and did just that while the chairman paced the room, coughed, then pulled up a seat.

He made himself comfortable, flicked the crease of his trousers into order, then, with a fatherly pat on the seat next to him, gestured Beryl to sit.

She obeyed.

Manifesto the Great's footman nodded and moved to his master. "Sir?"

"Yes, my good man."

"Is it barbecue time?" said Manifesto the Great's footman.

Manifesto the Great's face lit up. "Why yes, I think it is."

He stumbled; his footman caught him and led him away like an inebriated teenager. Beryl watched, not for the first time wondering if he had been drugged.

Every morning, Beryl walked into the room with a view to find a list an arm long on the whiteboard. Then, with controlled anger, she'd pick up a marker and cross out three, four, sometimes five with a clipped "done," then waited like Pavlov's dog for a reaction.

The chairman never disappointed; tormenting Beryl was the best part of the day, the proverbial cherry on a leadership cupcake, and she always rose to the bait.

But this morning, there was nothing—no glint in his eye, no list, and no readers around the table.

What the pickle was going on?

She waited for the chairman's usual sarcastic smile and cryptic comments, but there was nothing.

She looked at Manifesto the Great's footman stumbling out the door with the leader leaning against him like a drunk.

Manifesto the Great's footman mouthed "not now," which was as helpful as those stupid mechanical birds.

She sighed with no idea what to expect or what to do.

The chairman blew his nose, sniffed, then ruffled her head like she was one of those small mechanical four-legged creatures.

She shoved his hand away, waiting for a reaction.

Nothing.

Had he gotten someone else for his lists? Was there someone better than her?

How could there be? She knew every nook and cranny of things.

Instinct kicked in; her stomach knotted.

"Your project is now complete, congratulations," said the chairman.

"What?" said Beryl with her best blank face.

"There is nothing left to hide," he said.

"Oh."

She waited.

"So, what are we to do with you?" said the chairman.

She said nothing.

The chairman looked out of the window, sighed, then turned to Beryl. "You know so much."

"I can be of help to you," she said.

"But you're a woman," he said.

By the time the readers arrived, Beryl had been dismissed like a cleaner.

The "meeting," as the chairman called it, was pretty rubbish, hardly a meeting. To start, there was no one there but her and him—no records, minutes, or even a witness to protect her. And it was all one-sided, just him talking and her trying to read between the lines, and what she read made her heart sink.

Looking after the leader was not what she intended to do with her life.

She aspired to be a reader, to break through the whole "women are stupid" thing, but thanks to that friggin' chairman, that was as possible as the leader's footman wearing new trousers.

"You should be grateful," said the chairman. "I could've sent you to the institute for Petri dish filling."

Petri dish? thought Beryl.

She knew why she wasn't sent to the institute. It was full of cleaners, and she could talk.

"I have given you luxury caffeine on tap," said the chairman, "and a footman to pour it for you."

She said little.

The Librarian had warned, and Beryl had seen the backstabbing.

Over the years, she had seen the chairman cheese off half the population with his stupid rules. She had been laughed at, teased about her past, and she was smart enough to hide her feelings behind glasses and mousey hair to plot and plan.

She had no intention of failing, let alone being laughed at again.

She headed back to the basement.

She slid on her wig and looked in the mirror.

"Well, laugh this up, boys . . ." And, without a backward glance, she marched to Manifesto the Great's footman's room.

Manifesto the Great's footman looked up.

"Get me the cleaner," she said.

"The cleaner?" said Manifesto the Great's footman.

"Yes," said Beryl. "Her from the institute."

He stopped. "You mean *that* her?"

Beryl nodded.

Beryl had visited the institute many times, sneaking in late at night when no one was there and the Librarian was out for the count.

There was something about the babies that touched her, especially this new batch.

Once, she was almost caught and jumped behind the egg-popping station as a parade of carers appeared with a man.

They were naming the babies with stupid names, long and annoying. They stopped at one, a tiny, white-faced baby mesmerized by the aquarium of one fish.

"We're calling her Casandra Winthrop," boomed the man.

When they left, Beryl moved through the nursery, five of the babies peacefully sleeping in pods apart from the white-skinned one.

She was still staring at the fish aquarium.

Beryl touched her tiny button nose.

"When I'm in charge, we'll change that stupid name to something short and to the point—just like your nose."

She slid her finger into the palm of the baby's hand.

What a grip; she could crush a nut.

"You're a prodigy if ever there was one," laughed Beryl.

Manifesto the Great's footman's heart skipped a beat, breaking into a sort of fluttering that had him catching his breath. Beryl's future was as precarious as needlepoint balancing; should he advise or take a heart tablet?

Memories flooded back: Bette and the cleaners hated with a passion, and they were as volatile as leaking gas, TNT, or worse—a football mob.

He eyed Beryl's steely face; she was as determined as a hungry, wild, mechanical rat.

She looked back with an "it's now or never" look.

He clicked his heels and headed for the canteen.

About friggin' time, he told himself.

Chapter Twenty-Nine

MEMORIES

"The Petri was the great hope of many men whose women seemed to always have a headache."–Manifesto the Great

Manifesto the Great was sitting at the bottom of Arthur of the North's statue, or rather lounging across its big toe.

He liked to visit it; it reminded him of the elite days of ruling when he had a mum to argue with and LM-2 on his side. He sighed—all that hunting, shooting, and fishing (which shows how buggered his memory was, as he never did any).

He was knackered; he had spent all afternoon scraping graffiti into the toenail, giggling to himself.

"Big is as useful as a prick in a storm."

He loved the word *prick*; it always made him laugh. LM-2, too. What he wouldn't give to hear her laugh now. But she was gone, gone along with the last great turtle.

He paused. Wasn't it the turtle that crushed her? Or was that the other one?

His memory faded into the distance.

Not like his footman; *his* memory was as sharp as the beak of a mechanical bird, and his footman could pinpoint a moment in time as quick as said mechanical bird could peck.

Manifesto the Great decided he'd ask his footman about the turtle, perhaps get his quill out, write things down, and maybe even order him some new trousers.

He headed for the Building of Opulence's canteen; it was sunset, and his footman would be there sipping tea, his one good foot casually propped on a chair, entertaining the cleaners.

The canteen was a no-go area for footmen. They had changed sides before the coup had even started, and the cleaners never forgot—apart, that is, from Manifesto the Great's footman.

He was loyal.

According to Bette, he had more loyalty in his tooth's filling than all the other footmen put together, and the others agreed.

Manifesto the Great wandered into the canteen. The cleaners in the canteen didn't bat an eyelid; the leader "doing the queue" of the canteen was as common as a bird dropping on a statue.

They remembered the exact day when it started—when he first walked in for a "cuppa," fresh from scribbling on his father's statue.

It was right after the fall of the Librarian and that Fanny woman with the bras.

"Where have all the turtles gone?" he said. "I've been waiting all day."

"Sir, a turtle is not a taxi," said his footman, rising from his chair.

He made to "spirit" his leader away, but Manifesto the Great, captivated by the steaming mush from the hot food counter, joined the queue. He'd never seen mush before.

It was obvious he had been head-flattened, but secrecy was mandatory in the Building of Opulence. Every Building of Opulence worker had signed the "what happens in the building, stays in the building" treaty, and since the downfall of Fanny and the Librarian, all were too fearful of breaking it.

There were worse things than a mad leader to deal with, they told themselves, and sometimes, they believed it.

"I'll have what they are having," he said, and after a few mouthfuls, he never wanted to see it again—until the next day.

That was ten years ago, and every evening since, he appeared, spitting out his mush like it was the first time.

At first, those in the canteen hoped it would lead to something—at least to better food. In the end, they realized he was a leader in name only, and quite frankly, some of them were a little tired of the whole thing. After all, he went back to something better, something that required chewing; he could afford to "spit it out." They had to swallow or go hungry.

"Tell me what's happened to LM-2," he said, poised at the entrance like a lost child.

The cleaners looked at each other. "I'll get the tea," said the tall one.

The others nodded, ushering him to his usual seat.

The tall cleaner slid a mug down the table, Wild West style.

Manifesto the Great, caught up in the catching of it, forgot all about LM-2.

He blew on his excessively hot shit tea, then looked up. "Is there really no caffeine?"

"Ran out again, sir. Perhaps tomorrow," the short cleaner lied.

He sipped. "Well, I guess it is hot and steaming." He sipped again, this time attempting an "Arrrrgh."

"I've just been at the statue; the birds have been busy," he spluttered, forgetting about the graffiti.

The dishwasher looked up from her sink and sighed. "Another bit of friggin' scrubbing to do, again."

The leader looked about. "Where's my footman?"

The cleaners shrugged.

"I am looking for my quill," he said, brandishing a knife with a mad look.

With a gentle "here, sir," the short cleaner slid a pen into his hand while removing the knife.

He waited.

She slid a notepad beneath his pen.

"Start with Fanny," she said.

"Yes, yes," he mumbled. He wrote *Fanny* and stopped.

The cleaners waited.

"It was the bra," he muttered.

"Yes," muttered a few.

"Always the bra," said the short cleaner, now sweeping beneath his feet.

"You were out doing your speech," said the tall cleaner. "The 'things are going great' one."

"Me?"

"Yes, on your box. The one you stand on to see over the balcony."

"Oh, that; that's full of soap. I never use it now." He laughed to himself.

"You were always making speeches," said the dishwasher, collecting her statue-cleaning gear.

"Was I?" said Manifesto the Great.

"Until that Fanny fell. Then, well, you stopped."

"Thank the galaxies for that," said Manifesto the Great. "Can't have falling Fannys, can we?"

"Do you remember the drawing on the wall?" said the short cleaner.

The leader shook his head.

"Sure, you remember," said the dishwasher.

"I remember nothing." He gestured to the tea urn. "That rust bucket has more memory than me."

"No need to be so dramatic," said a voice from the back.

"Well, you try buttoning up things with no idea."

"The Librarian?" said the tall cleaner, skirting about his table with a damp cloth.

Manifesto the Great's face lit up as a memory flashed by.

The falling of Fanny, he wrote.

"That's it," said the tall cleaner.

He started to write.

Oblivious to the swish of cloth, the hoovering, the crash of a plate, the leader scribbled like a madman. Lost in his memories, he was deaf to the cleaners' banter, their jocular bin-emptying. He knew it would not be long before it was gone again, as quickly as he forgot why he came into the canteen in the first place.

"Penis," he mouthed, then stopped. Bugger. He looked up. "Where did I see that?"

The tall cleaner, with a crisp knot-tying of a bin bag, stopped. "Walls. Remember? Apparently, you recognized it before the others."

"It was but a poor artist," said a voice from the back, who considered bin-emptying beneath her.

"What the pickle is one of those doing on a wall?" said the leader; he stopped as he always did when it all came back to him.

He wrote, *The Mae West robot and my "things are going great" speech . . . the Librarian . . . wheelchair . . . flying . . . the elderly one.*

He stopped; no one could forget that image.

Manifesto the Great saw the Librarian soar across the street, the elderly reader hanging on like a flapping flag followed by a flock of prototypes.

Watching them go down was not something you would want to remember.

Nor the landing.

The wheelchair crashed at the foot of Arthur of the North's statue, scraping the "P" from a scribbled "prick," followed by the plop of the elderly reader and the Librarian.

The coup had finished before it started, before Manifesto the Great's footman even had a chance to shake a cocktail.

VERRUCA

"Looking the part is not the same as being the part."–Manifesto the Great's footman

When Fanny fell, she was taken to her home.

LM-2 and Maisie had no idea that Fanny had a girl, let alone that she had such an offensive name.

With no idea of how to explain procreation to a ten-year-old, LM-2 suggested a ceremonial burning of Fanny's leaflets.

Verruca, donning her mother's bra, jumped at the chance, vowing to keep her mother's memory alive.

"It's probably best not to," muttered Maisie. "It might go against you in the long run, a bit like your name."

"My mother called me this," she said. "Besides, if no one takes me seriously, then I can be of more help. Incognito-like."

LM-2 and Maisie looked at the string bean of a girl in orange.

Verruca, quickly reading their looks, said, "And as for this orange, who would suspect a girl in such bright colors? Besides, it's reversible, completely grey on the other side."

Bette was moping about the base of the watercooler, cursing the so-called educated institute workers. Their aim was on par with a blind three-year-old's. They spilled more water than a leaking tap and with no shame. She had seen them overfilling their cups with chilled water and blowing the overflow onto the floor, apart from Jack and John, who, out of respect, always half-filled their cups.

She, wringing a cloth into her bucket with a grunt, heard a rustle, followed by a familiar cough.

She looked up, catching sight of a note, just like in the good old days.

The days before she had been stripped of her manager title, assigned to watercooler duty, and told how lucky she was to keep her mop.

She picked it up, read it, and then, as ordered, ate it.

She almost smiled; she had never met this so-called PBO (purpose-built operator), but she had heard of Beryl. She sounded like the sort she could do business with, who could bring down those two-timing, double-crossing footmen, especially that good-for-nothing, sleazy oaf of a footman.

Bette working in the institute turned out to be a complete bonus for Beryl.

In fact, when Beryl suggested holding the first meeting in Jack and John's disused fertility shed, Bette wondered if she was being used.

Nobody went to the shed anymore, except to chuck out the unrecyclables, and as Bette cleared space for the meeting, she told herself to hold back, watch. She was still smarting from all those years back, when Manifesto the Great's footman turned against her.

That night, the shed filled up with women handpicked by Beryl.

Beryl had ideas but was unsure how to implement them, implementing not being her strong point.

She looked at the four women: the posh one, the tiny cleaner who insisted on bringing her friend, and Bette.

Beryl didn't know that many women, and she had even less experience dealing with them. She talked like a man with no sense of humor and how the city had gone to the "dogs."

"Dogs, what's that when it's at home?" said Tiny, pulling out a flask.

Beryl stopped; she never thought of refreshments. "Oh, it's an Earth thing," said the posh woman. "The readers love saying it: 'bed-diving has gone to the dogs,' 'the caffeine's gone to the dogs,' 'us women have gone to the dogs.'"

"I see." Tiny looked about the shed. "Any cups?"

"Fanny always talked of weapons of mass destruction, but never dogs," said the posh woman, dumping her beverage basket in front of the group.

"Yeah, and look what happened to her," said Tiny's friend.

"We need brains, not brawn," said Beryl.

"Yes, but overpowering with the Pythagorean Theorem is hardly gonna happen, is it?" said the posh woman.

The others looked at her with a "what?" apart from Bette; the Pythagorean Theorem was a piece of piss to her.

She stared at her trolley.

Here's me with more knowledge than a library, pushing that friggin' thing, mopping up after knobs of men, listening to their bozo-like ideas.

She shoved the trolley in disgust.

The trolley squeaked into action, bump-stopping at the picnic basket.

"Fanny always talked of surprise, the unexpected," said the posh woman.

"But she was mad," said Tiny's friend.

Bette stared at the trolley—so many compartments, even for the hoover.

She picked up the nozzle.

"No one would suspect one of these, let alone a trolley," she said.

"A trolley?" said Beryl.

"Or a duster," said Tiny.

The women looked at Tiny.

"One of those feathered ones with a stick. Some men think it's for tickling."

She blushed.

Bette looked at the women. "There is more to a hoover than sucking."

A few pulled a face.

"More to a feather duster than tickling," said Tiny, getting into the swing of things.

"We could load our equipment with explosives and really take 'em by surprise."

"Explosives? In a duster?" said Beryl.

"Well, at least it's better than the Pythagorean Theorem," muttered the posh woman.

Chapter Thirty-One

STARFISH

"A little incognito never harmed anyone."–Fanny

*B*eryl walked into the leader's office for her first day of "minding" to find the leader poised like a starfish, desperately trying to keep his balance.

She asked him what he was doing, and he mumbled, "Incognito."

"What's that when it's at home?" she said with her best smile.

"It's about not being seen," said Manifesto the Great.

She nodded like she understood and noticed that being poised like a starfish had the leader at his most vulnerable.

"Do all men practice this pose?" she said.

He shook his head with an "as if."

She laughed. "If mastered by many, you would have the beginnings of an army to protect from those dastardly Aliens."

His arms flopped to his side. "The Aliens are dastardly?"

Beryl shrugged. "Well, they could be."

Manifesto the Great nodded, confused.

"Why don't you make a morning thing of it, before your ablutions?" said Beryl.

"Ablutions?" He stopped and dropped to his chair.

"You could pass a law," said Beryl. "Make everyone do it."

The leader looked at her; she had lost him at "ablutions."

"You are the leader, aren't you?"

He nodded.

"Then why don't you lead?" said Beryl.

"Lead?" he said. "I can't even match my socks."

Beryl looked at the opened drawers, socks and underpants scattered everywhere, and began to pair them up. Manifesto the Great watched as she, with an eye for coordination, matched each pair with his underpants.

By the end of the morning, his wardrobe was color-coded and labeled, and Manifesto the Great followed Beryl about like a puppy, asking her questions of his past.

Beryl talked of LM-2 like she knew her personally, knew what happened to her; sourcing enough quills to write a novel, she even helped him record the story.

A story that had Manifesto the Great fussing over things like the turtles.

"LM-2 tried to save them," said Beryl. "Along with Maisie."

"Maisie?" he said, spelling "turtle" wrong.

"She's not important," muttered Beryl, correcting the missing "T."

When Manifesto the Great heard that LM-2 had become an outlaw, he almost cried until Beryl asked him to do his incognito pose. She even applauded when he made it past the ten-minute mark.

For weeks, Beryl worked on the leader, trying to find what made him tick, until she realized there was no tick to discover. His mind, like his diary, was as blank as the butt of a statue.

She sneaked out information while keeping him happy with pseudo bacon rolls, marveling at his incognito pose and filling him with caffeine, finally convincing him to pass the incognito bill.

It wasn't easy under the chairman's eye or that sleazy oaf of a footman's, but she did it.

"It was the caffeine," she told Bette.

"Oh?" Bette said.

"Caffeine from beans ripened under Earth's sun," she chuckled.

The cleaners pulled an "oh" face.

"And ground between the thighs of five Earth virgins—origins unknown."

"And what's a virgin when it's at home?" said the blonde cleaner.

"That's what he said," said Beryl.

"Aye, and this thigh malarky?" said Bette.

"It's a ruse," said the dark cleaner.

In truth, Beryl made the leader's caffeine from a packet in the canteen where all the other working girls made tea, which was where they were now, getting an update from "Herself," as Bette like to call Beryl.

The three cleaners watched as Beryl prepared the leader's brew in his special mug so precious some said it could only be cleaned with silk.

Beryl smiled to herself. Manifesto the Great had no idea his caffeine was as cheap as a worker's loo roll. He was too busy timing his pose, trying to beat his latest record. By the time he sipped his brew, it was cold and, with a quick sniff, followed by a toss, flying out the window, splattering on the heads of masses below.

Three tosses and Beryl, a frugal young woman, had changed his caffeine to something cheap, of recyclable origin, and—thinking of the masses—good for hair.

"A ruse?" said Bette.

"Yes," said Beryl. "It what all good spies do."

The readers were addicted to thirties films on the mirror, which, to be honest, was way more fun than listening to the ramblings of a pint-size leader, but when they saw the incognito pose, they downed their caffeine and laughed like never before.

"I am told it's good for the joints," said the leader.

The readers laughed louder, even the chairman.

"And don't tell me excellent for the libido," said a voice from the back.

"It could be," said Manifesto the Great, straightening his shirt over his potbelly.

"And what good is that without a woman happy to share it?" said the chairman, wiping tears of laughter from his eyes.

"I can promise the equipment but not the persuasion," said Manifesto the Great, pleased with his sentence.

The chairman looked around the room with a view; he had never seen them laugh before.

Perhaps a little incognito was what they needed.

Besides, there were rumors that it was possible to laugh a woman into bed.

The chairman looked at the oaf of a footman.

Although not proven to help the libido, the incognito pose became all the rage, marketed as the best thing since Wife-ie's yoga poses.

Within weeks, the incognito pose became a morning meditative ritual for men of a certain status, accompanied by a "hmmm."

It stretched everything, so many believed, and soon, there were contests to see how long a pose could be held.

It turned out that the leader found something he was great at.

Beryl could not believe how easy it was, and when Manifesto the Great's footman suggested bell-ringing to mark the beginning and end to "coordinate things," Beryl was bowled over.

"What a gem you are," she said.

Manifesto the Great's footman didn't answer; his hearing was as buggered as the leader's memory.

It was Bette's idea to "build up to the cleaning."

"Start with sweeping," she said to her girls, "then move on to polishing between the legs. Accustom the men." She smiled.

Besides, the women needed time to organize their equipment and practice their aim. The women's excitement was brewing; containing themselves was as easy as their target.

A hoover's aim is not brilliant, and as for a feather duster, it sprayed everywhere, exploding like a nail bomb.

Chapter Thirty-Two

MEDITATIONS AND BUNIONS

"Sometimes a ruler needs a gentle push of his perch."–LM-2

The bell-ringing was the last straw for the oaf of a footman. Nothing passed him; he could see there was more to this incognito pose than a "hmmm."

Every morning, he entered the room with a view to find the reader poised as a starfish with the cleaners quietly cleaning around them, dusting between their legs.

Many found the bustle of the cleaners soothing to their meditation.

"There is something about the swish of a duster," muttered the chairman, returning to his seat.

"I wouldn't trust a cleaner the length of a hoover," said the oaf of a footman.

Which had many confused.

The oaf of a footman was suspicious. "Why there?" he said, poised by the watercooler.

The two footmen looked at him like he was mad.

"What I wouldn't give for a woman on all fours down there," said the older one.

The younger footman said nothing.

"No wonder the men compete for length; I'd hold that pose all day for a woman on all fours."

"But they're cleaners," said the oaf of a footman.

"Exactly." The older footman chuckled.

"Don't you think it's a bit, well, suspicious?"

The younger footman stopped with a "come to think of it" look.

"Nah," said the older footman, "they're rolling it out for all men."

The oaf of a footman spluttered his water. "When?"

Manifesto the Great was working on his incognito pose when she appeared. Poised like a starfish with his potbelly pulsating in and out, he looked anything but the intellectual leader he used to be, and Beryl was impressed.

She was watching from the doorway, clutching his tray of caffeine.

She watched the so-called great leader struggle for balance.

"Why don't you try it on tippy-toes?" she said.

"What?" he said. "In these shoes?"

"Sir, you have no shoes on," said Beryl, gesturing to his bunions.

"Arrrrgh, yes, forgot about those little blighters."

He eased up onto his toes.

"Steady, steady."

He wobbled, fumbled, and grabbed his desk.

Beryl looked at the cleaner lurking about the doorway. "Not long now," she mouthed.

The cleaner, mid brushing of a cobweb, nodded, turned off her hoover, and whispered into the nozzle, "Tippy-toes in operation."

Beryl stared at her leader, trying to balance with his arms outstretched like a tightrope walker.

He smiled at Beryl.

"See, it works; incognito."

He wobbled again.

Any minute, thought Beryl with quick scrutiny of her nails.

He grabbed the desk and missed, sending the Leader of the Year paperweight ball skidding across the desk, straight for his manifesto notes.

Beryl feigned a save-the-notes run and made for the paperweight as Manifesto the Great tumbled to the floor.

"Bugger."

"It's now or never," shouted Beryl to the cleaner.

"Go, go, go," hissed the cleaner into her hoover nozzle.

Like a SWAT team in aprons, the cleaners descended into the offices, the corridors of power, and the canteen.

Manifesto the Great and his readers didn't stand a chance.

Chapter Thirty-Three

TNT

"Her mother was a servicer, which Beryl happily said until she realized what it meant."–The Librarian

The oaf of a footman saw it all.

Carrying a tray of empty glasses, he headed for the operations room.

The door was open.

A cleaner appeared, pushing a trolley with two men tied to it.

He stopped, flattened himself against the wall.

He peered around the corner, caught sight of an Operator bound and gagged with a cleaner behind. She had a mop pressed to his back, like a gun.

The Operator, catching sight of the oaf of a footman, gestured a "hide" with his eyebrows.

The oaf of a footman flattened himself behind the corner.

A mop?

He heard a bang and a crash, and he peered around the corner to see a hole where a wall once was.

"Was that absolutely necessary?" shouted a female voice.

Beryl? thought the oaf of a footman.

Bette appeared, her mop smoking. "He'll not make fun of my mop again," she said.

"Yes, well," said Beryl, appearing and clutching a tied-up Operator with a bag over his head, "if we are to rule, we need to use brains, not brawn."

"You? Rule?" said the muffled voice of the Operator. "Over my ingrown toenail."

Without even a backward glance, Beryl tossed him to a cleaner, who, swiftly attaching him to her trolley, headed down the corridor.

"It's not easy," he yelled. "Keeping a woman happy."

"That's because you are a man," shouted Bette, as Beryl disappeared back into the operation room.

"You damnable—" His muffled voice was followed by a scuffle, a thump, and silence.

"Right now, girls; let's clear up this mess," said Beryl. "Any word on the institute?"

The oaf of a footman pressed back behind his corner.

The institute?

He had his suspicions, but the institute?

He wondered if the chairman knew, wondered about a quick dash to the room with a view, when he heard a motorized stall and a squeal of brakes, followed by a crash and a string of swear words in a deep, posh, female voice coming from above.

The chairman.

He ran on his toes to the hidden stairs, two, three steps at a time, silently panting like his life depended on it.

At the top of the stairs, without even catching a breath, he creaked open the door a mere inch.

The chairman, bound and gagged, was on the floor in the foetal position, his face mashed into the shag pile and the Librarian's old wheelchair upturned, its wheel spinning.

A well-to-do woman stared at the fallen Operator and wiped her brow.

A cleaner appeared.

"What's he doing there?"

"The wheelchair's buggered," said the posh woman. "I mean, look at those wheels. The last time they saw a bit of grease, James the Strong was still alive and pulling spaceships."

"I told you to leave it in the skip."

"It's like pushing a pile of bricks," said the posh woman.

"What the spermicide is going on?" yelled a voice.

The women stopped as Bette marched into view. "He should be in rehab by now."

The oaf of a footman gulped. How did she move so quickly?

Bette glared at the spinning wheel. "Now is not the time for your pickling recycling."

Beryl appeared and flashed a looked at the stairs.

Manifesto the Great's footman shut the door, his "how" turning to "oh shit!"

"Where's that oaf of a footman?" she said.

Shit, shit, shit.

"That sleazy good-for-nothing. I'll find him," snapped Bette.

He headed back down the stairs three, four steps at a time, at high speed, raced into the basement, and stopped.

The locker room was open.

He crept closer, peered in, poised like a kung fu fighter, and dropped his arms.

The locker room was empty, with just the whiff of a fight like there had been a struggle.

He could hear men shouting, "Run away," "Head for the hills," "The hoovers are loaded," "Watch out for that duster."

He looked at the smear of blood on the shoe of his comrade; he had to get out of the city.

He slid through the back-alley door, his back flat against the wall, and peered into the street.

Women were pouring in from the market entrance, waving cleaning objects, stopping traffic, dragging men out of transporters, occasionally pointing a hoover or a feather duster, taunting any poor man that happened to get in the way.

"Take that," yelled a young woman, pointing a scrubbing brush at a transporter. The driver jumped out as his tire exploded.

Another blew up a streetlamp; a man threw himself into the bush.

It was terrifying.

Even more so when a bin exploded inches from him, spraying him with a taste like real steak packets.

The oaf of a footman squealed, and he was still shaking when a young Operator running by stopped.

Verruca was in her mother's old filing room at the time. It had taken her years to sort things out, and now empty as a pair of underpants on a line, she was pondering what to do next when her father barged in, slamming the door behind him.

"They're revolting," he said.

"What?" She looked at him.

"It's who, not what," he said.

She waited.

"The women," he said.

"I did warn you," said Verruca.

He paced the floor, wringing his hands. "You need to dress me up."

"With what?" said Verruca.

"I don't know." He ran his fingers through his hair. "Something of your mother's."

"I think there are still some bras somewhere," said Verruca.

"I need more than a bra," said her father.

She eyed him.

"I can make it to the Art Centre in a dress." He panted. "I heard there are few of us men there."

He stopped, his face filled with horror.

"Oh god, I heard they tie up men."

The oaf of a footman and the young footman with legs as long as a giraffe sprinted down the tunnel.

"Where the hell does this lead to?" said the oaf of a footman.

"I'm not sure, but I heard the Librarian used it." He paused for a moment. "Or was it Manifesto the Great's footman?"

Beryl looked about, the room with a view empty of men. She gave herself a moment to enjoy the pleasure and look out the window.

She stopped.

In the street below, strolling through the carnage, was a young woman wearing orange.

Beryl peered closer. She was with a man dressed as a woman and sporting the sort of chest that stopped traffic.

The young woman looked familiar.

"That's Fanny's daughter," said the posh woman. "I'd recognize that bra anywhere."

Within days, the city was empty of men, and the room with a view was full of women arguing over what to do.

Bette, despite her know-it-all approach to things, actually knew little about organizing and shouted a lot.

Beryl, with her speech prepared, was interrupted by the posh woman taking over.

Beryl saw herself as the leader, the main man, but everyone listened when the posh woman spoke. And when she talked of committees, voting, and ballot boxes, the women looked impressed.

"They call it socialism on Earth," she said. It turned out she was a friend of Fanny's in the good old days, when Fanny made sense.

Beryl decided to bide her time.

The posh woman was, after all, well past her prime.

THE BEGINNING OF THE END

"The men of Planet Hy Man believed in the power of the sperm— until the Petri dish came along."–The oaf of a footman

What was left of the men met in the Art Centre, a place the women had not touched.

They met in one of the old spaceships.

Verruca saw it all, and she was torn, at a loss at what to do, apart from perhaps giving up the orange suit.

Her father, an elderly man drained of energy, slumped in the corner of the spaceship while young men talked of how to win back what they had lost.

The oaf of a footman searched for someone he knew, a man like him, but those that had escaped were drivers, builders, and the odd reporter.

He felt ridiculous in his footman outfit.

The young footman laughed. "Just glad to be free," he said. "Easy to find a new pair of trousers."

The men talked of many things but struggled to find a leader.

The leggy footman watched; he knew the ins and outs of the Building of Opulence. "The women will soon miss us," he said.

No one believed him. Even the oaf of a footman thought he was an idiot—until, that is, the women not only took over but began to hunt down men.

The women made the city theirs; they argued and fought, struggling to find a leader.

Socialism, it seemed, was easier to spell than manage.

Beryl watched and waited while Verruca ventured into the outlands.

Verruca had never been to a campfire before, let alone sat by one; it was as her mother said—mesmerizing.

LM-2 handed her a hemp tea and Maisie a hemp smoke, and as the hemp soothed her, she smiled.

She knew there was more to come.

***

Would you like to read more?
Book 3 ***The Legacy Of Manifesto The Great***
is out now at your favourite store.
But don't race away just yet...
Turn the page for a taste of things to come

THE LEGACY OF MANIFESTO THE GREAT

Chapter One-The Footman's Outfit

"A man's underwear is not something you should have to face first thing in the morning."—Bette the Cleaner

1945

The day the city women took over the city was a day many tried to forget.

The city women went mad, rampaging like demented football fans —like wild dogs.

They raged in the streets, spilling into the lobby of the Building of Opulence, stopping at Hubby's statue. Realizing the pulling down of a statue was probably not a good idea, the women threw dusters instead, and when that felt good—underwear.

"Here, take that," yelled one.

"Yeah!" yelled another.

Until a woman, age undetectable, produced a spray can. Soon they were defacing on par with Fanny's "procreation graffiti."

Years of crap sex built up into the sort of crazed drawing of appendages that would have even a porn star blushing. Using every inflammatory word they could think of, they continued until the sun went down and James the Strong's massive thighs flashed onto the wall.

They stopped with breathless "where did that come from" looks; then, realizing it was merely a Hologram, they continued with their spray-painting.

The cleaners who had stormed the room with a view moved through the corridors, finally making their way to the footman's locker room.

They were heard before seen.

The oaf of a footman charged into the locker room. "They've got him," he shouted.

The footmen, mid changing, stopped.

"Who?" said one with a toss of his uniform.

"Manifesto the Great," said the oaf of a footman.

"Shit," said another.

"We're done for," screeched a voice from the shower.

"He told us to save ourselves," said the oaf of a footman. "'Head for the outlands,' he said, 'and don't look back.'"

"A legend," muttered one.

"A hero," sighed another.

The men emptied the locker room quicker than a bomb scare. So terrified were they, they took nothing, some were still in their underpants . . .

By the time the women entered, there was nothing. Just the odd shoe, the lockers ajar and the lingering aroma of something mannish: liniment, aftershave, with a hint of shoe polish.

The smell sent the women crazy.

They stripped the lockers, tossing silk pants and jackets into the air.

"Here, kitty kitty!" they jeered, laughing like crazy as shirts and trousers fluttered about them.

A middle-aged woman ripped off her apron, her shirt, and finally her bra.

The others stopped, silent, as the bra plopped to the ground like a pair of elephant ears.

She slid on a silk shirt with an "oooooh," stepped into a pair of trousers, and, with a wiggle, pulled the zip.

"Does my bum look big in this?" She glanced at a mirror.

The women were ecstatic; silk was as new to them as a man's groin. For years they had frumped around in aprons and itchy, floppy skirts, scrubbing things that required breath-holding. The silk smelt of aftershave, the trousers of something unfamiliar; inhaling was as pleasant as a decent cup of tea.

Soon they were strutting about, an easy thing to do in tight silky trousers.

"This is way better than an apron," said one.

"I feel like royalty," said another.

"A new look," yelled another.

Apart, that is, from Beryl.

She appeared mid locker upturning and yelled, "What the hell is going on here!"

The women stopped, saw it was some upstart twenty something minus an apron, and carried on.

"Leave 'em," said Bette, appearing beside her. "Years of picking up after the bigwigs can do that to a girl," she said.

"Bigwigs?" said Beryl.

"Yes," said Bette, eyeing up a costume herself. "That's what we called the Readers. These girls did all their dirty work, and I mean dirty work—these men didn't lift a finger when it came to cleaning."

She looked at Beryl.

"And a man's underwear is not something you should have to face first thing in the morning."

Beryl pulled a face.

She watched as five bigwig cleaners pulled on the footmen's outfits, slid on their wigs, and charged to the back alley, yelling, "Burn—burn!"

They piled their aprons about the garbage bins and, squealing like banshees, set the pile alight.

"Burn, burn!"

They taunted as mechanical rats, squealing at the top of their lungs, raced from the bins.

The women stamped on them, revealing in their power.

"We wear the pants now," yelled one.

"Yeah, take that!" stamped another as Bette, sporting Manifesto the Great's footman's extra-tight trousers, cheered them on.

Beryl said nothing. She had no apron and drew the line at a footman's wig.

But she had her own beehive hair, and she wasn't giving that up for anything . . .

Within weeks, the "bigwig" cleaners had taken over the room with a view like they took over the men.

Most of the men had been led away, stripped of their white coats, their prestige, their status, their precious caffeine. Only a few were held back to teach . . . including Jack and John.

It was all part of Bette's "transitory theory."

"If you can teach my girls, I will make it worth your while," she said. *Like they had a choice.*

Bette was at the helm, and she ruled like an overzealous born-again.

Bette, a woman whose apron betrayed her intelligence, had taken command, and with a swift tossing of her broom, she pranced about the room with a view, preaching like Billy Graham, not that anyone on Planet Hy Man knew who he was . . . yet.

Being a leader had really gone to her head.

Her first "there is more to a cleaner than disinfectant" speech went on all morning; it was longer than a Netflix serial.

"I learned many things in the shed," said Bette, "and if I can tell my egg from my spatula, so can anyone," putting a few off their morning caffeine.

"We are all pupils in life, just as we are all teachers," she said.

Some believed her, some had no idea what she was talking about, but all followed.

Bette was just so damn scary.

Now available at your favourite store

A NOTE FROM THE AUTHOR

I hope you enjoyed the rising of Manifesto Great. A stories inspired by my time living above an Indian restaurant and a huge need to use *Manifesto* in all it forms.
If you want to keep abreast of future Manifesto adventures then join me at...
www.kerrienoor.com

Or
Like me at...

facebook.com/kerrienoorwriter
twitter.com/kezzamac
instagram.com/kerrienoor

The Downfall Of Manifesto The Great

First edition. July 31, 2021.
Copyright © 2021 Kerrie Noor.
Written by Kerrie Noor.

❀ Created with Vellum